PEN

Three T
Ara

MALCOLM C. LYONS, sometime Sir Thomas Adams Professor of Arabic at Cambridge University and a life Fellow of Pembroke College, Cambridge, is a specialist in the field of classical Arabic literature. His published works include the biography *Saladin: the Politics of the Holy War*, *The Arabian Epic*, *Identification and Identity in Classical Arabic Poetry* and many articles on Arabic literature.

URSULA LYONS, formerly an Affiliated Lecturer at the Faculty of Oriental Studies at Cambridge University and, since 1976, an Emeritus Fellow of Lucy Cavendish College, Cambridge, specializes in modern Arabic literature.

ROBERT IRWIN is the author of *For Lust of Knowing: The Orientalists and Their Enemies*, *The Middle East in the Middle Ages*, *The Arabian Nights: A Companion* and numerous other specialized studies of Middle Eastern politics, art and mysticism. His novels include *The Limits of Vision*, *The Arabian Nightmare*, *The Mysteries of Algiers* and *Satan Wants Me*.

THREE TALES FROM THE ARABIAN NIGHTS

TRANSLATED BY MALCOLM C. LYONS AND URSULA LYONS
WITH AN INTRODUCTION BY ROBERT IRWIN

PENGUIN BOOKS

PENGUIN BOOKS

Published by the Penguin Group
Penguin Group (Australia)
250 Camberwell Road, Camberwell, Victoria 3124, Australia
(a division of Pearson Australia Group Pty Ltd)
Penguin Group (USA) Inc.
375 Hudson Street, New York, New York 10014, USA
Penguin Group (Canada)
90 Eglinton Avenue East, Suite 700, Toronto, Canada ON M4P 2Y3
(a division of Pearson Penguin Canada Inc.)
Penguin Books Ltd
80 Strand, London WC2R 0RL England
Penguin Ireland
25 St Stephen's Green, Dublin 2, Ireland
(a division of Penguin Books Ltd)
Penguin Books India Pvt Ltd
11 Community Centre, Panchsheel Park, New Delhi – 110 017, India
Penguin Group (NZ)
67 Apollo Drive, Rosedale, North Shore 0632, New Zealand
(a division of Pearson New Zealand Ltd)
Penguin Books (South Africa) (Pty) Ltd
24 Sturdee Avenue, Rosebank, Johannesburg 2196, South Africa

Penguin Books Ltd, Registered Offices: 80 Strand, London, WC2R 0RL, England

This translation first published 2008 .
This edition published by Penguin Group (Australia), 2010

1 3 5 7 9 10 8 6 4 2

Set in Monotype Dante
Typeset by Rowland Phototypesetting Ltd, Bury St Edmunds, Suffolk
Printed and bound in Australia by McPherson's Printing Group, Maryborough, Victoria

ISBN: 978-0-141-19468-4

penguin.com.au

FSC

Mixed Sources
Product group from well-managed
forests and other controlled sources
Cert no. SGS-COC-004121
www.fsc.org
© 1996 Forest Stewardship Council

Contents

Introduction

'*The Thousand and One Nights* is a marvel of Eastern literature', according to the Nobel Prize-winning Turkish novelist Orhan Pamuk. It is a book that has been familiar to him since childhood, but recently he decided to reread it, in order to understand why Western authors such as Stendhal, Coleridge, De Quincey and Poe were fascinated by these stories, and what made the book a classic. 'I saw it now as a great sea of stories – a sea with no end – and what astounded me was its ambition, its secret internal geometry . . . I was able finally to appreciate *The Thousand and One Nights* as a work of art, to enjoy its timeless games of logic, of disguises, of hide-and-seek, and its many tales of imposture.'*

It seems most probable that the core of the Arabic story collection *Alf Layla wa Layla*, 'The Thousand and One Nights' (also known in English as 'The Arabian Nights'), originated in ancient India. Then, sometime before the ninth century, these Sanskrit tales were translated into Persian under the title *Hazar Afsaneh* ('The Thousand Tales'), and doubtless Persian stories were added to this collection. By the ninth century at the latest, an Arabic version known as *The Book of the Story of a Thousand Nights* was in circulation. But *The Thousand and One Nights* in the

---

* Orhan Pamuk, *Other Colours: Essays and a Story* (London, 2007), pp. 121–2.

form we have it today, with its elaborate frame story about King Shahriyar and the storyteller Shahrazad, was compiled much later. The oldest substantially surviving manuscript of _The Thousand and One Nights_ seems to date from the fifteenth century. In the frame story – the 'Prologue' included in this volume – Shahrazad tells Shahriyar stories night after night in order to postpone her execution. The 'nights' function as story breaks. There are not actually a thousand and one stories. Some stories are very short, others very long. Some are about criminals, some about saints. Some feature magic and monsters, while others centre on commercial transactions or romantic assignations. It is the sheer variety of stories that gives the _Nights_ its unique quality.

Until quite recently these stories were not particularly esteemed in the Arab world. A French antiquarian and Orientalist, Antoine Galland, was chiefly responsible for their rediscovery and subsequent fame. In the years 1704 to 1717 he translated the stories in the oldest substantially surviving manuscript, and to this he added a translation of a manuscript of the Sinbad stories, as well as some stories that had been told to him by a Lebanese Christian. Galland's stories were an immediate success with French courtiers and intellectuals. The literary historian Paul Hazard has described how the craze for Shahrazad's story-telling replaced the slightly earlier craze for the traditional French fairy tales as rewritten by Charles Perrault: 'Then did the fairies Carabosse and Aurora make way for the throng of Sultanas, Viziers, Dervishes, Greek doctors, Negro slaves. Light fairylike edifices, fountains, pools guarded by lions of massy gold, spacious chambers hung with silks and tapestries from Mecca – all these replaced the palace where the beast had waited for Beauty to open her loving eyes.'*

Galland's French translation was itself swiftly translated into English and other languages. In the three centuries that followed there were several English translations of the *Nights* directly from the Arabic. The fullest of these was that made by the explorer and adventurer Sir Richard Burton, and published in ten volumes between 1885 and 1888. Burton based his translation on a version of the *Nights* that had been printed in Calcutta in the years 1839 to 1842.

A complete new translation of the *Nights* by Malcolm Lyons is now published by Penguin Classics in three volumes. This is the first translation into English since the 1880s of the fullest version of the *Nights*, that published in Calcutta, and it corrects Burton's errors in translation, as well as superseding his archaic and ugly prose style. This small selection of three tales brings together one story chosen from each of these volumes.

The 'Prologue', which sets the scene, can be and has been read as a profound fable about storytelling and its relationship to sex and death. 'Ali Baba' is one of the stories told to Galland by the Lebanese Christian. It is one of the most famous stories in the *Nights*. 'Judar and His Brothers' (Nights 606 to 624) is a strange tale of magic and betrayal. There is magic and treachery too in 'Ma'ruf the Cobbler' (Nights 989 to 1001), but also more comedy. These are indeed tales worthy to be 'written with needles on the inner corners of the eyeballs'.† Marvel and enjoy.

ROBERT IRWIN

---

* Paul Hazard, *The European Mind 1680–1715* (London, 1953), p. 411.
† From 'The Porter and the Three Ladies', volume 1.

Prologue

Among the histories of past peoples a story is told that in the old days in the islands of India and China there was a Sasanian king, a master of armies, guards, servants and retainers, who had two sons, an elder and a younger. Although both of them were champion horsemen, the elder was better than his brother; he ruled over the lands, treating his subjects with justice and enjoying the affection of them all. His name was King Shahriyar, while his younger brother, who ruled Persian Samarkand, was called Shah Zaman. For ten years both of them continued to reign justly, enjoying pleasant and untroubled lives, until Shahriyar felt a longing to see Shah Zaman and sent off his vizier to fetch him. 'To hear is to obey,' said the vizier, and after he had travelled safely to Shah Zaman, he brought him greetings and told him that his brother wanted a visit from him.

Shah Zaman agreed to come and made his preparations for the journey. He had his tents put up outside his city, together with his camels, mules, servants and guards, while his own vizier was left in charge of his lands. He then came out himself, intending to leave for his brother's country, but at midnight he thought of something that he had forgotten and went back to the palace. When he entered his room, it was to discover his wife in bed with a black slave. The world turned dark for him and he said to himself: 'If this is what happens before I have even left the city, what will this damned woman do if I spend time away with my brother?' So he drew his sword and struck, killing both his wife and her lover as they lay together, before going back and ordering his escort to move off.

When he got near to Shahriyar's city, he sent off messengers to give the good news of his arrival, and Shahriyar came out to meet him and greeted him delightedly. The city was adorned with decorations and Shahriyar sat talking happily with him, but Shah Zaman remembered what his wife had done and, overcome by sorrow, he turned pale and showed signs of illness. His brother thought that this must be because he had had to leave his kingdom and so he put no questions to him until, some days later, he mentioned these symptoms to Shah Zaman, who told him: 'My feelings are wounded,' but did not explain what had happened with his wife. In order to cheer him up, Shahriyar invited him to come with him on a hunt, but he refused and Shahriyar set off by himself.

In the royal palace there were windows that overlooked Shahriyar's garden, and as Shah Zaman was looking, a door opened and out came twenty slave girls and twenty slaves, in the middle of whom was Shahriyar's very beautiful wife. They came to a fountain where they took off their clothes and the women sat with the men. 'Mas'ud,' the queen called, at which a black slave came up to her and, after they had embraced each other, he lay with her, while the other slaves lay with the slave girls and they spent their time kissing, embracing, fornicating and drinking wine until the end of the day.

When Shah Zaman saw this, he told himself that what he had suffered was less serious. His jealous distress ended and, after convincing himself that his own misfortune was not as grave as this, he went on eating and drinking, so that when Shahriyar returned and the brothers greeted one another, Shahriyar saw that Shah Zaman's colour had come back; his face was rosy and, following his earlier loss of appetite, he was eating normally. 'You were pale, brother,' Shahriyar said, 'but now you have got your colour back, so tell me about this.' 'I'll tell you why I lost colour,' his brother replied, 'but don't press me to tell you how I got it back.' 'Let me know first how you lost it and became so weak,' Shahriyar asked him, and his brother explained: 'When you sent your vizier to invite me to visit you, I got ready and had gone out of the city when I remembered a jewel that was intended as a present for you, which I had left in my palace. I went back there to find a black slave sleeping in my bed with my wife, and it was after I had killed them both that I came on to you. I was full of concern about the affair and this was why I became pale and sickly, but don't make me say how I recovered.' Shahriyar, however, pressed him to do this, and so Shah Zaman finally told him all that he had seen.

'I want to see this with my own eyes,' said Shahriyar, at which Shah Zaman suggested that he pretend to be going out hunting again and then hide with him so that he could test the truth by seeing it for himself. Shahriyar immediately announced that he was leaving to hunt; the tents were taken outside the city and the king himself went out and took his seat in one of them, telling his servants that nobody was to be allowed in to visit him.

Then secretly he made his way back to the palace where his brother was and sat down by the window overlooking the garden. After a while the slave girls and their mistress came there with the slaves and they went on acting as Shah Zaman had described until the call for the afternoon prayer.

Shahriyar was beside himself and told his brother: 'Come, let us leave at once. Until we can find someone else to whom the same kind of thing happens, we have no need of a kingdom, and otherwise we would be better dead.' They left by the postern gate and went on for some days and nights until they got to a tall tree in the middle of a meadow, where there was a spring of water by the seashore. They drank from the spring and sat down to rest, but after a time the sea became disturbed and from it emerged a black pillar, towering up into the sky and moving towards the meadow. This sight filled the brothers with alarm and they climbed up to the top of the tree to see what was going to happen. What then appeared was a tall *jinni*, with a large skull and a broad breast, carrying a chest on his head. He came ashore and went up to sit under the tree on top of which the brothers were hiding. The *jinni* then opened the chest, taking from it a box, and when he had opened this too, out came a slender girl, as radiant as the sun, who fitted the excellent description given by the poet 'Atiya:

> She shone in the darkness, and day appeared
> As the trees shed brightness over her.
> Her radiance makes suns rise and shine,
> While, as for moons, she covers them in shame.
> When veils are rent and she appears,
> All things bow down before her.

As lightning flashes from her sanctuary,
A rain of tears floods down.

The *jinni* looked at her and said: 'Mistress of the nobly
born, whom I snatched away on your wedding night, I
want to sleep for a while.' He placed his head on her knee
and fell asleep, while she, for her part, looked up at the
tree, on top of which were the two kings. She lifted the
jinni's head from her knee and put it on the ground, before
gesturing to them to come down and not to fear him. 'For
God's sake, don't make us do this,' they told her, but she
replied: 'Unless you come, I'll rouse him against you and
he will put you to the cruellest of deaths.' This so alarmed
them that they did what they were told and she then said:
'Take me as hard as you can or else I'll wake him up.'
Shahriyar said fearfully to his brother: 'Do as she says.'
But Shah Zaman refused, saying: 'You do it first.'

They started gesturing to each other about this and the
girl asked why, repeating: 'If you don't come up and do
it, I'll rouse the *jinni* against you.' Because they were
afraid, they took turns to lie with her, and when they had
finished, she told them to get up. From her pocket she
then produced a purse from which she brought out a
string on which were hung five hundred and seventy
signet rings. She asked them if they knew what these were
and when they said no, she told them: 'All these belonged
to lovers of mine who cuckolded this *jinni*, so give me
your own rings.' When they had handed them over, she
went on: 'This *jinni* snatched me away on my wedding
night and put me inside a box, which he placed inside this
chest, with its seven heavy locks, and this, in turn, he put
at the bottom of the tumultuous sea with its clashing
waves. What he did not know was that, when a woman

wants something, nothing can get the better of her, as a poet has said:

> Do not put your trust in women
> Or believe their covenants.
> Their satisfaction and their anger
> Both depend on their private parts.
> They make a false display of love,
> But their clothes are stuffed with treachery.
> Take a lesson from the tale of Joseph,
> And you will find some of their tricks.
> Do you not see that your father, Adam,
> Was driven out from Eden thanks to them?

Another poet has said:

> Blame must be matched to what is blamed;
> I have grown big, but my offence has not.
> I am a lover, but what I have done
> Is only what men did before me in old days.
> What is a cause for wonder is a man
> Whom women have not trapped by their allure.'

When the two kings heard this, they were filled with astonishment and said to each other: '*Jinni* though he may be, what has happened to him is worse than what happened to us and it is not something that anyone else has experienced.' They left the girl straight away and went back to Shahriyar's city, where they entered the palace and cut off the heads of the queen, the slave girls and the slaves.

Every night for the next three years, Shahriyar would take a virgin, deflower her and then kill her. This led to unrest among the citizens; they fled away with their daughters until there were no nubile girls left in the city. Then, when the vizier was ordered to bring the king a girl as usual, he searched but could not find a single one, and had to go home empty-handed, dejected and afraid of what the king might do to him.

This man had two daughters, of whom the elder was called Shahrazad and the younger Dunyazad. Shahrazad had read books and histories, accounts of past kings and stories of earlier peoples, having collected, it was said, a thousand volumes of these, covering peoples, kings and poets. She asked her father what had happened to make him so careworn and sad, quoting the lines of a poet:

Say to the careworn man: 'Care does not last,
And as joy passes, so does care.'

When her father heard this, he told her all that had happened between him and the king from beginning to end, at which she said: 'Father, marry me to this man. Either I shall live or else I shall be a ransom for the children of the Muslims and save them from him.' 'By God,' he exclaimed, 'you are not to risk your life!' She insisted that it had to be done, but he objected: 'I'm afraid that you may experience what happened to the donkey and the bull with the merchant.' 'What was that,' she asked, 'and what happened to the two of them?' HER FATHER TOLD HER:

You must know, my daughter, that a certain merchant had both wealth and animals and had been given by Almighty God a knowledge of the languages of beasts and birds. He lived in the country and had at home a donkey and a bull. One day the bull went to the donkey's quarters and found them swept out and sprinkled with water; there was sieved barley and straw in his trough, while the donkey was lying there at his ease. At times his master would ride him out on some errand, but he would then be taken back.

One day the merchant heard the bull say to the donkey: 'I congratulate you. Here am I, tired out, while you are at your ease, eating sieved barley. On occasion the master puts you to use, riding on you but then bringing you back again, whereas I am always ploughing and grinding corn.' The donkey replied: 'When they put the yoke on your neck and want to take you out to the fields, don't get up, even if they beat you, or else get up and then lie down again. When they bring you back and put beans down for you, pretend to be sick and don't eat them; for one, two or three days neither eat nor drink and you will have a rest from your hard labour.'

The next day, when the herdsman brought the bull his supper, the creature only ate a little and next morning, when the man came to take the bull out to do the ploughing, he found him sick and said sadly: 'This was why he could not work properly yesterday.' He went to the merchant and told him: 'Master, the bull is unwell and didn't eat any of his food yesterday evening.' The merchant realized what had happened and said: 'Go and take the donkey to do the ploughing all day in his place.'

When the donkey came back in the evening after having been used for ploughing all day, the bull thanked him for his kindness in having given him a day's rest, to which the donkey, filled with the bitterest regret, made no reply. The next morning, the herdsman came and took him out to plough until evening, and when the donkey got back, his neck had been rubbed raw and he was half dead with tiredness. When the bull saw him, he thanked and praised him, but the donkey said: 'I was sitting at my ease, but was unable to mind my own business.' Then he went on:

'I have some advice to give you. I heard our master say that, if you don't get up, you are to be given to the butcher to be slaughtered, and your hide is to be cut into pieces. I am afraid for you and so I have given you this advice.'

When the bull heard what the donkey had to say, he thanked him and said: 'Tomorrow I'll go out with the men.' He then finished off all his food, using his tongue to lick the manger. While all this was going on, the merchant was listening to what the animals were saying. The next morning, he and his wife went out and sat by the byre as the herdsman arrived and took the bull out. When the bull saw his master, he flourished his tail, farted and galloped off, leaving the man laughing so much that he collapsed on the ground. His wife asked why, and he told her: 'I was laughing because of something secret that I saw and heard, but I can't tell you or else I shall die.' 'Even if you do die,' she insisted, 'you must tell me the reason for this.' He repeated that he could not do it for fear of death, but she said: 'You were laughing at me,' and she went on insisting obstinately until she got the better of him. In distress, he summoned his children and sent for the *qadi* and the notaries with the intention of leaving his final instructions before telling his wife the secret and then dying. He had a deep love for her, she being his cousin and the mother of his children, while he himself was a hundred and twenty years old.

When all his family and his neighbours were gathered together, he explained that he had something to say to them, but that if he told the secret to anyone, he would die. Everyone there urged his wife not to press him and so bring about the death of her husband and the father of her children, but she said: 'I am not going to stop until he tells me, and I shall let him die.' At that, the others stayed silent while the merchant got up and went to the byre to perform the ritual ablution, after which he would return to them and die.

The merchant had a cock and fifty hens, together with a dog, and he heard the dog abusing the cock and saying: 'You may be cheerful, but here is our master about to die.' When the cock asked why this was, the dog told him the whole story. 'By God,' exclaimed the cock, 'he must be weak in the head. I have fifty wives and I keep them contented and at peace while he has only one but still can't keep her in order. Why doesn't he get some mulberry twigs, take her into a room and beat her until she either dies or repents and doesn't ask him again?'

The vizier now said to his daughter Shahrazad: 'I shall treat you as that man treated his wife.' 'What did he do?' she asked, AND HE WENT ON:

When he heard what the cock had to say to the dog, he cut some mulberry twigs and hid them in a room, where he took his wife. 'Come,' he said, 'so that I can speak to you in here and then die with no one looking on.' She went in with him and he locked the door on her and started beating her until she fainted. 'I take it all back,' she then said, and she kissed his hands and feet, and after she had repented, she and her husband went out to the delight of their family and the others there. They lived in the happiest of circumstances until their deaths.

Shahrazad listened to what her father had to say, but she still insisted on her plan and so he decked her out and took her to King Shahriyar. She had given instructions to her younger sister, Dunyazad, explaining: 'When I go to the king, I shall send for you. You must come, and when you see that the king has done what he wants with me, you are to say: "Tell me a story, sister, so as to pass the waking part of the night." I shall then tell you a tale that, God willing, will save us.'

Shahrazad was now taken by her father to the king, who was pleased to see him and said: 'Have you brought what I want?' When the vizier said yes, the king was about to lie with Shahrazad but she shed tears and when he asked her what was wrong, she told him: 'I have a young sister and I want to say goodbye to her.' At that, the king sent for Dunyazad, and when she had embraced Shahrazad, she took her seat beneath the bed, while the king got up and deflowered her sister. They then sat talking and Dunyazad asked Shahrazad to tell a story to pass the waking hours of the night. 'With the greatest pleasure,' replied Shahrazad, 'if our cultured king gives me permission.' The king was restless and when he heard what the sisters had to say, he was glad at the thought of listening to a story and so he gave his permission to Shahrazad.

The Story of Ali Baba and the Forty Thieves Killed by a Slave Girl

SHAHRAZAD SAID TO SHAHRIYAR:

In a city of Persia, on the borders of your majesty's realms, there were two brothers, one called Qasim and the other Ali Baba. These two had been left very little in the way of possessions by their father, who had divided the inheritance equally between the two of them. They should have enjoyed an equal fortune, but fate was to dispose otherwise. Qasim married a woman who, shortly after their marriage, inherited a well-stocked shop and a warehouse filled with fine goods, together with properties and estates, which all of a sudden made him so well off that he became one of the wealthiest merchants in the city. By contrast, Ali Baba had married a woman as poor as himself; he lived in great poverty and the only work he could do to help provide for himself and his children was to go out as a woodcutter in a neighbouring forest. He would then load what he had cut on to his three donkeys – these being all that he possessed – and sell it in the city.

One day, while he was in the forest and had finished chopping just enough wood to load on to his donkeys, he noticed a great cloud of dust rising up in the air and advancing straight in his direction. Looking closely, he could make out a large crowd of horsemen coming swiftly towards him. Although there was no talk of thieves in the region, nonetheless it struck him that that was just what these could be. Thinking only of his own safety and not of what could happen to his donkeys, he climbed up into a large tree, where the branches a little way up were so densely intertwined as to allow very little space between them. He positioned himself right in the middle, all the more confident that he could see without being seen, as the tree stood at the foot of an isolated rock much higher than the tree and so steep that it could not be climbed from any direction.

The large and powerful-looking horsemen, well mounted and armed, came close to the rock and dismounted. Ali Baba counted forty of them and, from their equipment and appearance, he had no doubt they were thieves. He was not mistaken, for this was what they were, and although they had caused no harm in the neighbourhood, they had assembled there before going further afield to carry out their acts of brigandage. What he saw them do next confirmed his suspicions.

Each horseman unbridled his horse, tethered it and then hung over its neck a sack of barley which had been on its back. Each then carried off his own bag and most of these seemed so heavy that Ali Baba reckoned they must be full of gold and coins.

The most prominent of the thieves, who seemed to be their captain, carried his bag like the rest and approached the rock close to Ali Baba's tree. After he had made his way through some bushes, this man was clearly heard to utter the following words: 'Open, Sesame.' No sooner had he said this than a door opened, and after he had let all his men go in before him, he too went in and the door closed.

The thieves remained for a long time inside the rock. Ali Baba was afraid that if he left his tree in order to escape, one or all of them would come out, and so he was forced to stay where he was and to wait patiently. He was tempted to climb down and seize two of the horses, mounting one and leading the other by the bridle, in the hope of reaching the city driving his three donkeys in front of him. But, as he could not be sure what would happen, he took the safest course and remained where he was.

At last the door opened again and out came the forty thieves. The captain, who had gone in last, now emerged first; after he had watched the others file past him, Ali Baba heard him close the door by pronouncing these words: 'Shut, Sesame.' Each thief returned to his horse and remounted, after bridling it and fastening his bag on to it. When the captain finally saw they were all ready to depart, he took the lead and rode off with them along the way they had come.

Ali Baba did not climb down straight away, saying to himself: 'They may have forgotten something which would make them return, and were that to happen, I would be caught.' He looked after them until they went out of sight, but he still did not get down for a long time afterwards until he felt completely safe. He had remembered the words used by the captain to make the door open and shut, and he was curious to see if they would produce the same effect for him. Pushing through the shrubs, he spotted the door which was hidden behind them, and going up to it, he said: 'Open, Sesame.' Immediately, the door opened wide.

He had expected to see a place of darkness and gloom and was surprised to find a vast and spacious manmade chamber, full of light, with a high, vaulted ceiling into which daylight poured through an opening in the top of the rock. There he saw great quantities of foodstuffs and bales of rich merchandise all piled up; there were silks and brocades, priceless carpets, and, above all, gold and coins in heaps or heaped up in sacks or in large leather bags that were piled one on top of the other. Seeing all these things, it struck him that for years, even centuries, the cave must have served as a refuge for generation upon generation of thieves. He had no hesitation about what to do next: he entered the cave and immediately the door closed behind him, but that did not worry him, for he knew the secret of how to open it again. He was not interested in the rest of the money but only in the gold coins, particularly those that were in the sacks, so he removed as much as he could carry away and load on to his three donkeys. He next rounded up the donkeys, which had wandered off, and when he had brought them up to the rock he loaded them with the sacks, which he hid by arranging firewood on top of them. When he had finished, he stood in front of the door and as soon as he uttered the words 'Shut, Sesame', the door closed, for it had closed by itself each time he had gone in and had stayed open each time he had gone out.

Having done this, Ali Baba took the road back to the

city, and when he got home, he brought the donkeys into a small courtyard, carefully closing the door behind him. He removed the small amount of wood which covered the sacks and these he then took into the house, putting them down and arranging them in front of his wife, who was sitting on a sofa.

She felt the sacks and, realizing they were full of money, she suspected him of having stolen it. So when he had finished bringing them all to her, she could not help saying to him: 'Ali Baba, you can't have been so wicked as to . . . ?' 'Nonsense, wife!' Ali Baba interrupted her. 'Don't be alarmed: I'm not a thief, or at least only a thief who robs thieves. You will stop thinking ill of me when I tell you about my good fortune.' He then emptied the sacks, making a great heap of gold which quite dazzled his wife, and having done this, he told her the story of his adventure from beginning to end. When he had finished, he told her to keep everything secret.

Once his wife had recovered from her fright, she rejoiced with her husband at the good fortune which had come to them and she wanted to count all the gold that was in front of her, coin by coin. 'Wife,' said Ali Baba, 'that's not very clever: what do you think you are going to do and how long will it take you to finish counting? I am going to dig a trench and bury the gold there; we have no time to lose.' 'But it would be good if we had at least a rough idea of how much there is there,' she told him. 'I'll go and borrow some small scales from the neighbours and use them to weigh the gold while you are digging the trench.' Ali Baba objected: 'There is no point in that, and, believe me, you should leave well alone. However, do as you like, but take care to keep the secret.'

To satisfy herself, however, Ali Baba's wife went out

to the house of her brother-in-law, Qasim, who lived not very far away. Qasim was not at home and so, in his absence, she spoke to his wife, asking her to lend her some scales for a short while. Her sister-in-law asked her if she wanted large scales or small scales, and Ali Baba's wife said she wanted small ones. 'Yes, of course,' her sister-in-law replied. 'Wait a moment and I will bring you some.' The sister-in-law went off to look for the scales, which she found, but knowing how poor Ali Baba was and curious to discover what sort of grain his wife wanted to weigh, she thought she would carefully apply some candle grease underneath them, which she did. She then returned and gave them to her visitor, apologizing for having made her wait and saying she had had difficulty finding them.

When Ali Baba's wife got home, she placed the scales by the pile of gold, filled them and then emptied them a little further away on the sofa, until she had finished. She was very pleased to discover how much gold she had weighed out and told her husband, who had just finished digging the trench.

Whilst Ali Baba was burying the gold, his wife, in order to show her sister-in-law how meticulous and correct she was, returned her scales to her, not noticing that a gold coin had stuck to the underside of the scales. 'Dear sister-in-law,' she said to her as she returned them to her, 'you see, I didn't keep your scales very long. I'm bringing you them back, and I'm very grateful to you.' As soon as her back was turned, Qasim's wife looked at the underside of the scales and was astonished beyond words to find a gold coin stuck there. Immediately her heart was filled with envy. 'What!' she exclaimed. 'Ali Baba has gold enough to be weighed! And where did the wretch get it from?'

As we have said, her husband, Qasim, was not at home

but in his shop, from which he would only get back in the evening. So the time she had to wait for him seemed like an age, so impatient was she to tell him news which would surprise him no less than it had surprised her. When Qasim did come home, his wife said to him: 'Qasim, you may think you are rich, but you are wrong; Ali Baba has infinitely more than you; he doesn't count his money, like you – he weighs it!' Qasim demanded an explanation of this mystery and she then proceeded to enlighten him, telling him of the trick she had used to make her discovery; and she showed him the gold coin that she had found stuck to the underside of the scales – a coin so ancient that the name of the prince stamped on it was unknown to him.

Qasim, far from being pleased at his brother's good fortune, which would relieve his misery, conceived a mortal jealousy towards him and scarcely slept that night. The next morning, before even the sun had risen, he went to his brother, whom he did not treat as a real brother, having forgotten the very word since he had married the rich widow. 'Ali Baba,' he said, 'you don't say much about your affairs; you act as though you were poor, wretched and poverty-stricken but yet you have gold enough to weigh!' 'Brother,' replied Ali Baba, 'I don't know what you are talking about. Explain yourself.' 'Don't pretend to be ignorant,' said Qasim, showing him the gold coin his wife had handed to him. 'How many more coins do you have like this one, which my wife found stuck to the underside of the scales that your wife came to borrow yesterday?'

On hearing this, Ali Baba realized that, thanks to his wife's persistence, Qasim and his wife already knew what he had been so eager to keep concealed; but the damage was done and could not be repaired. Without showing the least sign of surprise or concern, he admitted everything to his brother and told him by what chance he had discovered the thieves' den and where it was, offering to give him a share in the treasure if he kept the secret. 'I will indeed claim my share,' said Qasim arrogantly, then added: 'But I also want to know precisely where this treasure is, the signs and marks of its hiding place, and how I can get in if I want to; otherwise, I shall denounce you to the authorities. If you refuse, not only will you have no hope of getting any more of it, but you will lose what you have already removed, as this will be given to me for having denounced you.' Ali Baba, more thanks to his own good nature than because he was intimidated by the insolent threats of so cruel a brother, told him everything he wanted to know, even the words to use when entering or leaving the cave.

Qasim asked no more questions but left, determined to get to the treasure before Ali Baba. Very early the next morning, before it was even light, he set out, hoping to get the treasure for himself alone. He took with him ten mules carrying large chests which he planned to fill, and he had even more chests in reserve for a second trip, depending on the number of loads he found in the cave. He took the path following Ali Baba's instructions and, drawing near to the rock, he recognized the signs and the tree in which Ali Baba had hidden. He looked for the door, found it, and said 'Open, Sesame' to make it open. When it did, he went in, and immediately it closed again. Looking around the cave, he was amazed at the sight of riches far greater than Ali Baba's account had led him to expect. The more closely he examined everything, the more his astonishment increased. Being the miser he was and fond of wealth and riches, he would have spent the whole day feasting his eyes on the sight of so much gold had he not remembered that he had come to remove it and load it on to his ten mules. He then took as many sacks as he could carry and went to open the door, but his mind was filled with thoughts far removed from what should have been of more importance to him. He found he had forgotten the necessary word and so instead of saying 'Open, Sesame', he said 'Open, Barley' and was very surprised to see that the door, rather than opening, remained shut. He went on naming various other types of grain, but not the one he needed, and still the door did not open.

Qasim had not expected this. In the great danger in which he found himself, he was so terror-stricken that, in his efforts to remember the word 'Sesame', his memory became more and more confused and soon it was as though he had never ever heard of the word. He threw down his sacks and began to stride around the cave from one side to another, no longer moved by the sight of all the riches around him. So let us now leave Qasim to bewail his fate – he does not deserve our compassion.

Towards midday, the thieves returned to their cave, and when they were a little way off, they saw Qasim's mules by the rock, laden with chests. Disturbed by this unusual sight, they advanced at full speed, scaring away the ten mules, which Qasim had neglected to tether. They had been grazing freely, and they now scattered so far into the forest that they were soon lost from sight. The thieves did not bother to run after them – it was more important for them to discover their owner. While some of them went round the rock to look for him, the captain, together with the rest, dismounted and went straight to the door, sword in hand; he pronounced the words and the door opened.

Qasim, who had heard the sound of the horses from the middle of the cave, was in no doubt that the thieves had arrived and that his last hour had come. Resolved at least to make an effort to escape from their hands and save himself, he was ready to hurl himself through the door immediately it opened. As soon as he saw it open and hearing the word 'Sesame', which he had forgotten, he rushed out headlong, flinging the captain to the ground. But he did not escape the other thieves who were standing sword in hand and who killed him on the spot.

After they had killed him, the first concern of the thieves was to enter the cave. Next to the door they found the sacks which Qasim had begun to carry off in order to load on to his mules. These they put back in their place, failing to notice what Ali Baba had previously removed. They consulted each other and discussed what had just happened, but although they could see how Qasim might have got out of the cave, what they could not imagine was how he had entered it. It struck them that he might have come down through the top of the cave, but there was nothing to show that this was what he had done, and the opening which let in the daylight was so high up and the top of the rock so inaccessible from outside that they all agreed it was incomprehensible. They could not believe that he had come in through the door, unless he knew the secret of making it open, and they were certain that no one else knew this. In this they were mistaken, unaware as they were that Ali Baba had found it out by spying on them.

They then decided that, however it was that Qasim had managed to get into the cave, it was now a question of protecting their communal riches and so they should chop his body in four and place the four pieces inside the cave near the door, two on each side, so as to terrify anyone who was bold enough to try the same thing. They themselves would only come back some time later, when the stench of the corpse had passed off. They carried out their plan, and as there was nothing else to keep them there, they left their den firmly secured, remounted their horses and went off to scour the countryside along the caravan routes, attacking and carrying out their usual highway robberies.

Qasim's wife, meanwhile, was in a state of great anxiety when she saw that night had come and her husband had not returned home. In her alarm, she went to Ali Baba and said to him: 'Brother-in-law, I believe you know well enough that your brother, Qasim, went to the forest and you know why he went there. He hasn't come back yet and as it has been dark for some time, I'm afraid that some misfortune may have befallen him.'

After the conversation that Ali Baba had had with his brother, he had suspected that he would make this trip into the forest and so he had not gone there himself that day so as not to alarm him. Without reproaching his visitor in any way which could cause offence to her or to her husband, if he was alive, he told her not to be worried yet, explaining that Qasim might well have thought fit not to come back to the city until well after dark.

Qasim's wife believed him all the more readily when she realized how important it was that her husband should act in secret. So she went home and waited patiently until midnight, but after that her fears increased and her suffering was all the more intense because she could not give vent to it nor relieve it by crying out loud, for she knew well enough that the reason for it had to remain concealed from the neighbours. The damage had been done, but she repented the foolish curiosity and blameworthy impulse which had led her to meddle in the affairs of her in-laws. She spent the night in tears, and as soon as it was light, she rushed to Ali Baba's house and told him and his wife – more through her tears than her words – what had brought her there.

For his part, Ali Baba did not wait for his sister-in-law to appeal to his kindness to find out what had happened to Qasim. Telling her to calm down, he then immediately set out with his three donkeys and made for the forest. He found no trace of his brother or of the ten mules along the way, but when he drew near the rock, he was astonished to see a pool of blood near the door. He took this for an evil omen and, standing in front of the door, he pronounced the words 'Open, Sesame'. When the door opened, he was confronted by the sorry sight of his brother's corpse, cut into four pieces. Forgetting what little fraternal love his brother had shown him, he did not hesitate in deciding to perform the last rites for his brother. He made up two bundles from the body parts that he found in the cave and these he loaded on to one of his donkeys, with firewood on top to conceal them. Then, losing no more time, he loaded the other two donkeys with sacks filled with gold, again with firewood on top, as before. As soon as he had done this and had commanded the door to shut, he set off on the path leading back to the city, but he took the precaution of stopping long enough at the edge of the forest so as to enter it only when it was dark. When he arrived home, he brought in only the two donkeys laden with the gold, leaving his wife with the job of unloading them. He told her briefly what had happened to Qasim, before leading the other donkey to his sister-in-law's house.

When he knocked at the door, it was opened by Marjana. Now this girl Ali Baba knew to be a very shrewd and clever slave who could always find a way to solve the most difficult of problems. When he had entered the courtyard, Ali Baba unloaded the firewood and the two bundles from the donkey and, taking Marjana aside, said to her: 'Marjana, the first thing I am going to ask you is an inviolable secret – you will see how necessary this is for us both, for your mistress as well as for myself. In these two bundles is the body of your master; he must be buried as though he died a natural death. Let me speak to your mistress, and listen carefully to what I say to her.'

After Marjana had told her mistress that he was there, Ali Baba, who had been following her, entered and his sister-in-law immediately cried out impatiently to him: 'Brother-in-law, what news have you of my husband? Your face tells me you have no comfort to offer me.' 'Sister-in-law,' replied Ali Baba, 'I can't tell you anything before you first promise me you will listen to me, from beginning to end, without saying a word. It is no less important to you than it is to me that what has happened should be kept a deadly secret, for your good and your peace of mind.' 'Ah!' exclaimed Qasim's wife, although without raising her voice. 'You are going to tell me that my husband is dead, but at the same time I must control myself and I understand why you are asking me to keep this a secret. So tell me; I am listening.'

Ali Baba told his sister-in-law what had happened on his trip, right up to his return with Qasim's body, adding: 'This is all very painful for you, all the more so because you so little expected it. However, although the evil

cannot be remedied, if there is anything capable of comforting you, I offer to marry you and join the little God
has given me to what you have. I can assure you that my
wife won't be jealous and you will live happily together.
If you agree, then we must think how to make it appear
that my brother died of natural causes: this is something
it seems to me you can entrust to Marjana, and I for my
part will do everything that I can.'

What better decision could Qasim's widow take than
to accept Ali Baba's proposal? With all the wealth she had
inherited through the death of her first husband she had
yet found someone even wealthier than herself, a husband
who, thanks to the treasure he had discovered, could
become richer still. So she did not refuse his offer but, on
the contrary, considered the match as offering reasonable
grounds for consolation. The fact that she wiped away the
copious tears she had begun to shed and stifled the piercing
shrieks customary to the newly widowed made it clear
enough to Ali Baba that she had accepted his offer.

He left her in this frame of mind and returned home
with his donkey, after having instructed Marjana to carry
out her task as well as she could. She, for her part, did her
best and, leaving the house at the same time as Ali Baba,
she went to a nearby apothecary's shop. She knocked on
the door and when it was opened she went in and asked
for some kind of tablets which were very effective against
the most serious illnesses. The apothecary gave her what
she had paid for, asking who was ill in her master's house.
'Ah!' she sighed heavily. 'It's Qasim himself, my dear
master! They don't know what's wrong with him; he
won't speak and he won't eat.' So saying, she went off
with the tablets – which Qasim was in no state to use.

The next morning, Marjana again went to the same

apothecary and, with tears in her eyes, asked for an essence which one usually gives the sick only when they are at death's door. 'Alas!' she cried in great distress as the apothecary handed it to her. 'I am very much afraid that this remedy will have no more effect than the tablets! Ah, that I should lose such a good master!'

For their part, Ali Baba and his wife could be seen, with sorrowful faces, making frequent trips all day long to and from Qasim's house, so that it was no surprise to hear, towards evening, cries and lamentations coming from Qasim's wife, and especially from Marjana, which told of Qasim's death.

Very early the next day, when dawn was just breaking, Marjana left the house and went to seek out an elderly cobbler on the square who, as she knew, was always the first to open his shop every day, long before everyone else. She went up to him, greeted him and placed a gold coin in his hand. Baba Mustafa, as he was known to all and sundry, being of a naturally cheerful disposition and always ready with a joke, looked carefully at the coin because it was not yet quite light and, seeing it was indeed gold, exclaimed: 'That's a good start to the day! What's all this for? And how can I help you?' 'Baba Mustafa,' Marjana said to him, 'take whatever you need for sewing and come with me immediately, but I will have to blindfold you when we reach a certain place.'

When he heard this, Baba Mustafa became squeamish, saying: 'Aha! So you want me to do something that goes against my conscience and my honour?' Placing another gold coin in his hand, Marjana went on: 'God forbid that I should ask you to do anything which you couldn't do in all honour! Just come, and don't be afraid.'

The man allowed himself to be led by Marjana, who,

after she had placed a handkerchief over his eyes at the place she had indicated, took him to the house of her late master, only removing the handkerchief once they were in the room where she had laid out the body, each quarter in its proper place. When she had removed the handkerchief, she said to him: 'Why I have brought you here is so that you can sew these pieces together. Don't waste any time, and when you have done this, I will give you another gold coin.'

When Baba Mustafa had finished, Marjana blindfolded him once more in the same room and then, after having given him the third gold coin that she had promised him, telling him to keep the secret, she took him back to the place where she had first blindfolded him. There she removed the handkerchief and let him return to his shop, watching him until he was out of sight in order to stop him retracing his steps out of curiosity to keep an eye on her.

She had heated some water with which to wash the body, and Ali Baba, who arrived just after she returned, washed it, perfumed it with incense and then wrapped it in a shroud with the customary ceremonies. The carpenter brought the coffin which Ali Baba had taken care to order, and Marjana stood at the door to receive it, to make sure that the carpenter would not notice anything. After she had paid him and sent him on his way, she helped Ali Baba to put the body into the coffin, and when Ali Baba had firmly nailed down the planks on top of it, she went to the mosque to give notice that everything was ready for the burial. The people at the mosque whose business it was to wash the bodies of the dead offered to come and perform their duty, but she told them it had already been done.

No sooner had Marjana returned than the imam and

the other officials of the mosque arrived. Four neighbours had assembled there who then carried the bier on their shoulders to the cemetery, following the imam as he recited the prayers. Marjana, as the dead man's slave, followed bare-headed, weeping and wailing pitifully, violently beating her breast and tearing her hair. Ali Baba also followed, accompanied by neighbours who would step forward from time to time to take their turn to relieve the four who were carrying the bier, until they arrived at the cemetery.

As for Qasim's wife, she stayed at home grieving and uttering pitiful cries with the women of the neighbourhood who, as was the custom, hurried there whilst the funeral was taking place, adding their lamentations to hers and filling the whole quarter and beyond with grief and sadness. In this way, Qasim's grisly death was carefully concealed and covered up by Ali Baba, his wife, Qasim's widow and Marjana, so that no one in the town knew anything about it or was in the least suspicious.

Three or four days after the funeral, Ali Baba moved the few items of furniture he had, together with the money he had taken from the thieves' treasure – which he brought in only at night – to the house of his brother's widow in order to set up house there. This was enough to show that he had now married his former sister-in-law, but no one showed any surprise, as such marriages are not unusual in our religion.

As for Qasim's shop, Ali Baba had a son who some time ago had finished his apprenticeship with another wealthy merchant who had always testified to his good conduct. Ali Baba gave him the shop, with the promise that if he continued to behave well, he would soon arrange an advantageous marriage for him, in keeping with his status.

Let us now leave Ali Baba to start enjoying his good fortune, and talk about the forty thieves. When they returned to their den in the forest at the time they had agreed on, they were astonished first at the absence of Qasim's body but even more so by the noticeable gaps among their piles of gold. 'We've been discovered, and if we don't take care we'll be lost,' said the captain. 'We must do something about this immediately, for otherwise bit by bit we shall lose all the riches which we and our fathers amassed with so much trouble and effort. What our loss teaches us is that the thief whom we surprised learned the secret of how to make the door open and that fortunately we arrived at the very moment he was going to come out. But he wasn't the only one – there must be someone else who found out about this. Quite apart from anything, the fact that the corpse was removed and some of our treasure taken is clear proof of this. There is nothing to show that more than two people knew the secret, however, and so now that we have killed one of them we shall have to kill the other as well. What do you think, my brave men? Isn't that what we should do?'

The band of thieves were in complete accord with their captain, and finding his proposal perfectly reasonable, they all agreed to abandon any other venture and to concentrate exclusively on this and not to give up until they had succeeded. 'I expected no less of your courage and bravery,' their captain told them. 'But before anything else, one of you who is bold, clever and enterprising must go to the city, unarmed and dressed as a traveller from foreign parts. He is to use all his skill to discover if there is any talk about the strange death of the wretch we so rightly slaughtered, in order to find out who he was and where he lived. That's what is most important for us to know, so that we don't do anything we might regret or show ourselves in a country where for a long time no one has known about us and where it is very important for us to stay unknown. Were our volunteer to make a mistake and bring back a false report rather than a true one, this could be disastrous for us. Don't you think, then, that he had better agree that, if he does this, he should be killed?'

Without waiting for the rest to vote on this, one of the thieves said: 'I agree and I glory in risking my life by taking on this task. If I don't succeed, remember at least that, for the common good of the band, I lacked neither the good-will nor the courage.' He was warmly praised by the captain and his comrades, after which he then disguised himself in such a way that no one would take him for what he was. Leaving his comrades behind, he set out that night and saw to it that he entered the city as day was just breaking. He made for the square, where the one shop that he found open was that of Baba Mustafa.

Baba Mustafa was seated on his chair, his awl in his hand, ready to ply his trade. The robber went up to him to bid him good morning and, seeing him to be of great age, said to him: 'My good fellow, you start work very early, but you cannot possibly see clearly at your age, and even when it gets lighter, I doubt that your eyes are good enough for you to sew.' 'Whoever you are,' replied Baba Mustafa, 'you obviously don't know me. However old I may seem to you, I still have excellent eyes and you will realize the truth of this when I tell you that not long ago I sewed up a dead man in a place where the light was hardly any better than it is at the moment.' The thief was delighted to find that after his arrival he had come across someone who, as seemed certain, had, immediately and unprompted, given him the very information for which he had come.

'A dead man!' the thief exclaimed in astonishment, adding, in order to make him talk: 'What do you mean, "sewed up a dead man"? You must mean that you sewed the shroud in which he was wrapped?' 'No, no,' insisted Baba Mustafa, 'I know what I mean. You want to make me talk, but you're not going to get anything more out of me.'

The thief needed no further enlightenment to be persuaded that he had discovered what he had come to look for. Pulling out a gold coin, he placed it in Baba Mustafa's hand, saying: 'I don't want to enter into your secret, although I can assure you that I would not reveal it if you confided it to me. The only thing I ask is that you be kind enough to tell me or show me the house where you sewed up the dead man.' 'Even if I wanted to, I could not,' replied Baba Mustafa, ready to hand back the gold coin. 'Take my word. The reason is that I was led to a certain place where I was blindfolded and from there I let myself be taken right into the house. When I had finished what I had to do, I was brought back in the same way to the same place, and so you see that I cannot be of any help to you.' 'You ought at least to remember something of the path you took with your eyes blindfolded,' the thief went on. 'Come with me, I beg you, and I will blindfold you in that place, and we will go on together by the same path, taking the turns that you can remember. As every effort deserves a reward, here is another gold coin. Come, do me the favour I ask of you.' On saying this, he placed another gold coin in his hand.

Baba Mustafa was tempted by the two gold coins; he gazed at them in his hand for a while without uttering a word, thinking over what he should do. Finally, he pulled out a purse from his breast and put them there, saying to the thief: 'I can't guarantee I will remember the precise path I was led along, but since that's what you want, let's go. I will do what I can to remember it.'

To the thief's great satisfaction, Baba Mustafa rose and, without closing his shop – where there was nothing of consequence to lose – he led the thief to the place where Marjana had blindfolded him. When they arrived there, he said: 'Here is where I was blindfolded and I was turned like this, as you see.' The thief, who had his handkerchief ready, bound his eyes and then walked beside him, sometimes leading him and sometimes letting himself be led, until he came to a halt. 'I don't think I went any further,' said Baba Mustafa, and indeed he was standing before Qasim's house where Ali Baba was now living. Before he removed the handkerchief from his eyes, the thief quickly put a mark on the door with a piece of chalk which he had ready in his hand. He then removed it and asked Baba Mustafa if he knew to whom the house belonged. But Baba Mustafa replied that he could not tell him as he was not from that quarter. Seeing that he could not learn anything more, the thief thanked him for his trouble, and after he had left him to return to his shop, he himself took the path back to the forest, certain that he would be well received.

Shortly after the two of them had parted, Marjana came out of Ali Baba's house on some errand and when she returned, she noticed the mark the thief had made and stopped to examine it. 'What does this mark mean?' she asked herself. 'Does someone intend to harm my master, or is it just children playing? Well, whatever the reason, one must guard against every eventuality.' So she took a piece of chalk and, as the two or three doors on either side were similar, she marked them all in the same spot and then went inside, without telling her master or mistress what she had done.

The thief, meanwhile, had gone on until he had reached the forest, where he quickly rejoined his band. He told them of his success, exaggerating his good luck in finding right at the start the only man who would have been able to tell him what he had come to discover. They listened to what he said with great satisfaction and the captain, after praising him for the care that he had taken, addressed them all. 'Comrades,' he said, 'we have no time to lose; let us go, well armed but without making this too obvious. We must enter the town separately, one after the other, so as not to arouse suspicion, and meet in the main square, some of us coming from one side, some from the other. I myself will go and look for the house with our comrade who has just brought us such good news, in order to decide what we had better do.'

The thieves applauded their captain's speech and were soon ready to set out. They went off in twos and threes, and by walking at a reasonable distance from one another, they entered the town without arousing any suspicions. The captain and the thief who had gone there that morning were the last of them. The latter led the captain to the street where he had marked Ali Baba's house, and on coming to one of the doors which had been marked by Marjana, he pointed it out to him, telling him that that was the house. However, as they continued on their way without stopping so as not to look suspicious, the captain noticed that the next door had the same mark in the same spot. When he pointed this out to his companion and asked him if that was the door or the first one, the other was confused and did not know what to reply. His confusion increased when the two of them saw that the next four or five doors were marked in the same way. The scout swore to the captain that he had marked only one door, adding: 'I don't know who can have marked the others all in the same way, but I admit that I am too confused to be sure which is the one I marked.' The captain, seeing his plan had come to nothing, went to the main square and told his men through the first man he encountered that all their trouble had been wasted: their expedition had been useless and all they could do now was to return to their den in the forest. He led the way and they all followed in the same order in which they had set out.

When they had reassembled in the forest, he explained to them why he had made them come back. With one voice, they all declared that the scout deserved to be put to death; and indeed, he even condemned himself by admitting that he should have taken greater precautions, stoically offering his neck to the thief who came forward to cut off his head.

Since the preservation of the group meant that the wrong that had been done to them should not go unavenged, a second thief, who vowed he would do better, came forward and asked to be granted the favour of carrying out their revenge. They did this and he set out. Just as the first thief had done, he bribed Baba Mustafa, who, with his eyes blindfolded, showed him where Ali Baba's house was. The thief put a red mark on it in a less obvious spot, reckoning that this would surely distinguish the house from those which had been marked in white. But a little later, just as she had done on the day before, Marjana came out of the house and, when she returned, her sharp eyes did not fail to spot the red mark. For the same reasons as before, she made the same mark with red chalk in the same spot on all the other doors on either side.

The scout, on returning to his companions in the forest, made a point of stressing the precaution he had taken which, he claimed, was infallible and would ensure that Ali Baba's house could not be confused with the rest. The captain and his men agreed with him that this would succeed, and they made for the city in the same order, taking the same precautions as before, armed and ready to pull off the planned coup. When they arrived, the captain and the scout went straight to Ali Baba's street but encountered the same difficulty as before. The captain was indignant, while the scout found himself as confused as his predecessor had been. The captain was again forced to go back with his men, as little satisfied as on the previous day, and the scout, as the man responsible for the failure, suffered the same fate, to which he willingly submitted himself.

The captain, seeing how his band had lost two of its brave men, was afraid that more still would be lost and his band would diminish further if he continued to rely on others to tell him where the house really was. The example of the two made him realize that on such occasions his men were far better at using physical force rather than their heads. So he decided to take charge of the matter himself and went to the city, where Baba Mustafa helped him in the same way as he had helped the other two. He wasted no time placing a distinguishing mark on Ali Baba's house but examined the place very closely, passing back and forth in front of it several times so that he could not possibly mistake it.

Satisfied with his expedition and having learned what he wanted to find out, he went back to the forest. When he reached the cave where his band was waiting for him, he addressed them, saying: 'Comrades, nothing can now stop us from exacting full vengeance for the harm that has been done to us. I now know for sure the house of the man on whom revenge should fall, and on my way back I thought of such a clever way of making him experience it that no one will ever again be able to discover our hideaway or where our treasure is. This is what we have to aim for, as otherwise, instead of being of use to us, the treasure will be our downfall. To achieve this, here is what I thought of and if, when I finish explaining it, any one of you can think of a better way, he can tell us.' He went on to explain to them what he intended to do; and as they had all given him their approval, he then told them to disperse into the towns, surrounding villages and even the cities, where they were to buy nineteen mules and thirty-eight leather jars for transporting oil, one full of oil and the others empty.

Within two or three days, the thieves had collected all these. As the empty jars were a little too narrow at the top, the captain had them widened. Then, after he had made one of his men enter each of the jars, with such weapons as he thought they needed, he left open the sections of the jars that had been unstitched to allow each man to breathe freely. After that he closed them in such a way that they appeared to be full of oil. To disguise them further, he rubbed them on the outside with oil taken from the filled jar.

When all this had been done, the mules were loaded with the thirty-seven thieves – not including the captain – each hidden in one of the jars, together with the jar which was filled with oil. With the captain in the lead, they took the path to the city at the time he had decided upon and arrived at dusk, about one hour after the sun had set, as he had planned. He entered the city and went straight to Ali Baba's house, with the intention of knocking on the door and asking to spend the night there with his mules, if the master of the house would agree to it. He had no need to knock for he found Ali Baba at the door, enjoying the fresh air after his supper. After he brought his mules to a halt, the captain said to Ali Baba: 'Sir, I have come from far away, bringing this oil to sell tomorrow in the market. I don't know where to stay at this late hour, so if it is not inconvenient to you, would you be so kind as to let me spend the night here? I would be very obliged to you.' Although in the forest Ali Baba had seen the man who was now speaking to him and had even heard his voice, how could he have recognized him as the captain of the forty thieves in his disguise as an oil merchant? 'You are very welcome, come in,' he replied, standing aside to let him in with his mules. When the man had entered, Ali Baba summoned one of his slaves and ordered him to put the mules under cover in the stable after they had been unloaded, and to give them hay and barley. He also took the trouble of going to the kitchen and ordering Marjana quickly to prepare some supper for the guest who had just arrived and to make up a bed for him in one of the rooms.

Ali Baba did even more to make his guest as welcome as possible: when he saw that the man had unloaded his mules, that the mules had been led off into the stable as he had ordered, and that he was looking for somewhere to spend the night in the open air, he went up to him in the hall where he received guests, telling him he would not allow him to sleep in the courtyard. The captain firmly refused his offer of a room, under the pretext of not wishing to inconvenience him, although in reality this was so as to be able to carry out what he planned in greater freedom, and he only accepted the offer of hospitality after repeated entreaties.

Not content with entertaining someone who wanted to kill him, Ali Baba went on to talk with him about things which he thought would please him, until Marjana brought him his supper, and he left his guest only when he had eaten his fill, saying: 'I will leave you as the master here; you have only to ask for anything you need: everything in my house is at your disposal.' The captain got up at the same time as Ali Baba and accompanied him to the door, and while Ali Baba went into the kitchen to speak to Marjana, he entered the courtyard under the pretext of going to the stable to see if his mules needed anything. Ali Baba once more told Marjana to take good care of his guest and to see he lacked for nothing, adding: 'I am going to the baths early tomorrow morning. See that my bath linen is ready – give it to Abdullah; and then make me a good beef stew to eat when I return.' Having given these orders, he then retired to bed.

Meanwhile, the captain came out of the stable and went to tell his men what they had to do. Beginning with the man in the first jar and carrying on until the last, he said to each one: 'As soon as I throw some pebbles from the room in which they have put me, cut open the jar from top to bottom with the knife you have been given and, when you come out, I shall be there.' The knives he meant were pointed and had been sharpened for this purpose.

He then returned and Marjana, seeing him standing by the kitchen door, took a lamp and led him to the room which she had prepared for him, leaving him there after having asked him if there was anything else he needed. Soon afterwards, so as not to arouse any suspicion, he put out the lamp and lay down fully dressed, ready to get up as soon as he had taken a short nap.

Marjana, remembering Ali Baba's orders, prepared his bath linen and gave it to the slave Abdullah, who had not yet gone to bed. She then put the pot on the fire to prepare the stew, but while she was removing the scum, her lamp went out. There was no more oil in the house nor were there any candles. What should she do? She had to see clearly to remove the scum, and when she told Abdullah of her quandary, he said to her: 'Don't be so worried: just take some oil from one of the jars here in the courtyard.'

Marjana thanked him for his advice and while he went off to sleep near Ali Baba's room so as to be ready to follow him to the baths, she took the oil jug and went into the courtyard. When she approached the first jar she came across, the thief hidden inside it asked: 'Is it time?' Although the man had spoken in a whisper, Marjana could easily hear his voice because the captain, as soon as he had unloaded his mules, had opened not only this jar but also all the others, to give some air to his men who, though they could still breathe, had felt very uncomfortable. Any other slave but Marjana, surprised at finding a man in the jar instead of the oil she was looking for, would have caused an uproar that could have done a lot of harm. But Marjana was of superior stock, immediately realizing the importance of keeping secret the pressing danger which threatened not only Ali Baba and his family but also herself. She grasped the need to remedy the situation swiftly and quietly, and thanks to her intelligence, she saw at once how this could be done. Restraining herself and without showing any emotion, she pretended to be the captain and replied: 'Not yet, but soon.' She went up to the next jar and was asked the same question, and she went on from jar to jar until she reached the last one, which was full of oil, always giving the same reply to the same question. In this way she discovered that her master, Ali Baba, who thought he was merely offering hospitality to an oil merchant, had let in to his house thirty-eight thieves, including the bogus oil merchant, their captain. Quickly filling her jug with oil from the last jar, she returned to the kitchen where she filled the lamp with the oil and lit it. She then took a large cooking pot and returned to the courtyard where she filled it with oil from the jar and brought the pot back and put it over the fire. She put plenty of wood underneath because the sooner the pot boiled the sooner she could carry out her plan to save the household, as there was no time to spare. At last the oil boiled; taking the pot, she went and poured enough boiling oil into each jar, from the first to the last, to smother and kill the thieves – and kill them she did.

This deed, which was worthy of Marjana's courage, was quickly and silently carried out, as she had planned, after which she returned to the kitchen with the empty pot and closed the door. She put out the fire she had lit, leaving only enough heat to finish cooking Ali Baba's stew. Finally, she blew out the lamp and remained very quiet, determined not to go to bed before watching what happened next, as far as the darkness allowed, through a kitchen window which overlooked the courtyard.

She had only to wait a quarter of an hour before the captain awoke. He got up, opened the window and looked out. Seeing no light and as the house was completely quiet, he gave the signal by throwing down pebbles, several of which, to judge by the sound, fell on the jars.

He listened but heard nothing to tell him that his men were stirring. This worried him and so he threw some more pebbles for a second and then a third time. They fell on the jars and yet not one thief gave the least sign of life. He could not understand why and, alarmed by this and making as little noise as possible, he went down into the courtyard. When he went up to the first jar, intending to ask the thief, whom he thought to be alive, whether he was asleep, he was met by a whiff of burning oil coming from the jar. He then realized that his plan to kill Ali Baba and pillage his house and, if possible, carry back the stolen gold had failed. He moved on to the next jar and then all the others, one after the other, only to discover that all his men had perished in the same way. Then, on seeing how the jar which he had brought full of oil had been depleted, he realized just how he had lost the help he had been expecting. In despair at the failure of his attempt, he slipped through Ali Baba's garden gate, which led from the courtyard, and made his escape by passing from garden to garden over the walls.

After she had waited a while, Marjana, hearing no further sound and seeing that the captain had not returned, was in no doubt about what he had decided to do, as he had not tried to escape by the house door which was locked with a double bolt. She went to bed at last and fell asleep, delighted and satisfied at having so successfully ensured the safety of the whole household.

Ali Baba, meanwhile, set out before daybreak and went to the baths, followed by his slave, quite unaware of the astonishing events which had taken place in his house while he was asleep. For Marjana had not thought that she should wake him and tell him about them, as she had quite rightly realized she had no time to lose at the moment of danger and that it was pointless to disturb him after the danger had passed.

By the time Ali Baba had returned home from the baths, the sun had already risen, and when Marjana came to open the door for him, he was surprised to see that the jars of oil were still in their place and that the merchant had not gone to the market with his mules. He asked her why this was, for Marjana had left things just as they were for him to see, so that the sight of them could explain to him more effectively what she had done to save him. 'My good master,' Marjana replied, 'may God preserve you and all your household! You will understand better what you want to know when you have seen what I have to show you. Please come with me.' Ali Baba followed her and, after shutting the door, she led him to the first jar. 'Look inside,' she said, 'and see if there is any oil there.' Ali Baba looked, but seeing a man in the jar, he drew back in fright, uttering a loud cry. 'Don't be afraid,' said Marjana. 'The man you see won't do you any harm. He has done some damage but is no longer in a condition to do any more, either to you or to anyone else – he's no longer alive.' 'Marjana,' exclaimed Ali Baba, 'what is all this that you have just shown me? Explain to me.' 'I will tell you,' she replied, 'but control your astonishment and don't stir up the curiosity of your neighbours, lest they find out something that is very important for you to keep secret. But come and see the other jars first.'

Ali Baba looked into the other jars one after the other, from the first to the last one, in which he could see that the oil level was now much lower. After looking, he stood motionless, saying not a word but staring now at the jars, now at Marjana, so great was his astonishment. At last, as if he had finally recovered his speech, he asked: 'But what has become of the merchant?' 'The merchant,' replied Marjana, 'is no more a merchant than I am. I will tell you who he is and what has become of him. But you will learn the full story more comfortably in your own room, as it's time, for the sake of your health, to have some stew after your visit to the baths.'

While Ali Baba returned to his room, Marjana went to the kitchen to fetch the stew. When she brought it to him, he said to her before eating it: 'Satisfy my impatience and tell me this extraordinary story at once and in every detail.'

Obediently, Marjana began: 'Master, last night, when you had gone to bed, I prepared your linen for the bath, as you had told me, and I gave it to Abdullah. I then put the stew pot on the fire, but while I was removing the scum, the lamp suddenly went out for lack of oil. There was not a drop of oil left in the jug, and so I went to look for some candle ends but couldn't find any. Seeing me in such a fix, Abdullah reminded me of the jars in the court-yard which we both believed, as you did yourself, were full of oil. I took the jug and ran to the nearest one, but when I got to it, a voice came from inside, asking: "Is it time?" I wasn't startled, for I realized at once the bogus merchant's malicious intent, and I promptly replied: "Not yet, but soon." I went to the next jar and a second voice asked me the same question, to which I gave the same reply. I went from jar to jar, one after the other, and each time came the same question and I gave the same answer. It was only in the last jar that I found any oil and I filled my jug from it. When I considered that there were thirty-seven thieves in the middle of your courtyard, just waiting for the signal from their captain – whom you had taken for a merchant and had received so warmly – to set your house alight, I lost no time. I took the jar, lit the lamp and, taking the largest cooking pot in the kitchen, I went and filled it with oil. I put the pot over the fire and when the oil was boiling hot, I went and poured some into each of the jars where the thieves were. This was enough to stop them carrying out their plan to destroy us, and when my plan succeeded, I went back to the kitchen and put out the lamp. Then, before going to bed, I quietly went and stood by the window to see what the bogus oil merchant would do. A short time later, I heard him throw some pebbles from his window down on to the jars, as a signal. He did this twice or thrice and then, as he could neither see nor hear any movement coming from below, he came down and I saw him go from jar to jar, until after he had reached the last one, I lost sight of him because of the darkness. I kept watch for some time after that and, when he didn't return, I was sure he must have escaped through the garden, in despair at his failure. Convinced that the household was now quite safe, I went to bed.'

Having completed her account, Marjana added: 'This is the story you asked me to tell you and I am certain it all follows from something I noticed two or three days ago which I didn't think I needed to tell you. Early one morning, as I came back from the city, I saw that there was a white mark on our street door and next day there was a red mark next to it. I didn't know why this was and so on both occasions I went and marked two or three doors next to us up and down the street in the same way and in the same spot. If you add this to what has just happened, you will see that it was all a plot by the thieves of the forest who, for some reason, have lost two of their number. Be that as it may, they have now been reduced to three, at the most. This goes to show that they have

sworn to do away with you and that you had better be on
your guard as long as we can be sure that there is even
one left alive. For my part,' she concluded, 'I will do
everything I can to watch over your safety, as is my duty.'

When she had finished, Ali Baba, realizing how much
he owed to her, said: 'I will not die before rewarding you
as you deserve, for I owe my life to you. As a token of my
gratitude, I shall start by giving you your freedom as of
this moment, until I can reward you properly in the way
I have in mind. I, too, am persuaded that the forty thieves
set this ambush up for me, but through your hands God
has saved me. May He continue to preserve me from their
wickedness, and by warding off their wickedness from me,
may He deliver the world from their persecution and their
vile breed. What we must now do is immediately to bury
the bodies of these pests of the human race, in complete
secrecy, so that no one will suspect what has happened.
That's what I'm going to work on with Abdullah.'

Ali Baba's garden was very long and at the end of it
were some large trees. Without further delay, he went
with Abdullah and together they dug a trench under the
trees, long enough and wide enough for all the bodies
they had to bury. The earth was easy to work, so that the
job was soon completed. They then pulled the bodies out
of the jars and, after removing the weapons with which
the thieves were armed, they took the bodies to the
bottom of the garden and laid them in the trench. After
they had covered them with the soil from the trench, they
scattered the rest of it around so that the ground seemed
the same as before. Ali Baba carefully hid the oil jars and
the weapons; while, as for the mules, for which he had no
further use, he sent them at different times to the market,
where he got his slave to sell them.

While Ali Baba was taking all these measures to stop people discovering how he had become so rich in such a short time, the captain of the thieves had returned to the forest in a state of unimaginable mortification. In his agitation, confused by so unexpected a disaster, he returned to the cave, having come to no decision about how or what he should or should not do to Ali Baba.

The solitude in which he found himself in this place seemed horrible to him. 'Brave lads,' he cried out, 'companions of my vigils, my struggles and adventures, where are you? What will I do without you? Have I chosen you and collected you together only to see you perish all at once by a fate so deadly and so unworthy of your courage? Had you died sword in hand like brave men, I would regret your death. When will I ever be able to get together another band of hardy men like you again? And even if I wanted to, could I do so without exposing so much gold, silver and riches to the mercy of someone who has already enriched himself with part of it? No, I could not and should not think of it before I have first got rid of him. I shall do by myself what I have not been able to do with such powerful assistance. When I have seen to it that this treasure is no longer exposed to being plundered, I will ensure that after me it will stay neither without successor nor without a master; rather, that it may be preserved and increase for all posterity.' Having made this resolution, he did not worry about how to carry it out; and so, full of hope and with a quiet mind, he went to sleep and spent a peaceful night.

The next morning, having woken up very early as he had intended, he put on new clothes of a kind suitable for his plan and went to the city, where he took up lodgings in a *khan*. Expecting that what had happened at Ali Baba's

house might have caused some uproar, he asked the
doorkeeper in the course of his conversation what news
there was in the city, to which the doorkeeper replied by
telling him all sorts of things, but not what he needed
to know. From that, he decided that Ali Baba must be
guarding his great secret because he did not want the fact
that he knew about the treasure and how to get to it to
be spread abroad. Ali Baba, for his part, was well aware
that it was for this reason that his life was in jeopardy.

This encouraged the captain to do everything he could
to get rid of Ali Baba by the same secret means. He
provided himself with a horse and used it to transport to
his lodgings various kinds of rich cloths and fine fabrics
which he brought from the forest in several trips, taking
the necessary precautions to conceal the place from where
he was taking them. When he had got what he thought
enough, he looked for a shop and having found one, he
hired it from the proprietor, filled it with his stock and
established himself there. Now the shop opposite this one
used to belong to Qasim and had recently been occupied
by Ali Baba's son. The captain, who had taken the name
of Khawaja Husain, soon exchanged courtesies with the
neighbouring merchants, as was the custom. Since Ali
Baba's son was young and handsome and did not lack
intelligence, the captain frequently had occasion to speak
to him, as he did to the other merchants, and soon made
friends with him. He even took to cultivating him more
assiduously when, three or four days after he had established himself there, he recognized Ali Baba, who had
come to see his son and talk with him, as he did from
time to time. He later learned from the son, after Ali Baba
had left, that this was his father. So he cultivated him
all the more, flattered him and gave him small gifts,

entertaining him and on several occasions inviting him to eat with him.

Ali Baba's son did not want to be under so many obligations to Khawaja Husain without being able to return them. But his lodgings were cramped and he was not well off enough to entertain him as he wished. He talked about this to his father, pointing out to him that it was not proper to let Khawaja Husain's courtesies remain unrecognized for much longer.

Ali Baba was delighted to take on the task of entertaining him himself. 'My son,' he said, 'tomorrow is Friday. As it is a day when the big merchants like Khawaja Husain and yourself keep their shops closed, arrange to take a stroll with him after dinner; when you return, arrange it so that you bring him past my house and make him come in. It's better to do it this way than if you were to invite him formally. I shall go and order Marjana to prepare the supper and have it ready.'

On Friday, Ali Baba's son and Khawaja Husain met after dinner at their agreed rendezvous and went on their walk. As they returned, Ali Baba's son carefully made Khawaja Husain pass down the street where his father lived, and when they came to the house door, he stopped and said to him, as he knocked: 'This is my father's house. When I told him about the friendship with which you have honoured me, he told me to see to it that you honoured him with your acquaintance. I beg you to add this pleasure to all the others for which I am already indebted to you.' Although Khawaja Husain had got what he wanted, which was to enter Ali Baba's house and murder him without endangering his own life and without causing a stir, nevertheless he made his excuses and pretended to be about to take leave of the son. But as Ali

Baba's slave had just opened the door, the son seized him by the hand and, going in first, pulled him forcibly after him, as if in spite of himself.

Ali Baba met Khawaja Husain with a smiling face and gave him all the welcome he could wish for. He thanked him for the kindness he had shown to his son, adding: 'The debt he and I owe you is all the greater, since he is a young man still inexperienced in the ways of the world and you are not above helping instruct him in these.' Khawaja Husain returned the compliment by assuring him that though some old men might have more experience than his son, the latter had enough good sense to serve in place of the experience of very many others.

After talking for a short while on unimportant matters, Khawaja Husain wanted to take his leave, but Ali Baba stopped him, saying: 'My dear sir, where do you want to go? Please do me the honour of dining with me. The meal I would like to offer you is much inferior to what you deserve but, such as it is, I hope that you will accept it in the same spirit in which I offer it to you.' 'Dear sir,' Khawaja Husain rejoined, 'I know you mean well. If I ask you not to think ill of me for leaving without accepting this kind offer of yours, I beg you to believe me that I don't do this out of disrespect or discourtesy. I have a reason which you would appreciate, if you knew it.' 'And may I ask what this can be?' said Ali Baba. 'Yes, I can tell you what it is: it is that I don't eat meat or stew which contains salt. Just think how embarrassed I would be, eating at your table.' 'If that's the only reason,' Ali Baba replied, 'it should not deprive me of the honour of having you to supper, unless you wish it. First, there's no salt in the bread which we have in my house; and as for the meat and the stews, I promise you there won't be any in what will be served you. I shall go and give the order, and so, please be good enough to stay, as I shall be back in a moment.'

Ali Baba went to the kitchen and told Marjana not to put any salt on the meat she was going to serve and immediately to prepare two or three extra stews, in addition to those he had ordered, and these were to be unsalted. Marjana, who was ready to serve the meal, could not stop herself showing annoyance at this new order and having it out with Ali Baba. 'Who is this awkward fellow, who doesn't eat salt? Your supper will no longer be fit to eat if I serve it later.' 'Don't be angry, Marjana,' Ali Baba continued. 'He's perfectly all right. Just do as I tell you.'

Marjana reluctantly obeyed, and, curious to discover who this man was who did not eat salt, when she had finished and Abdullah had set the table, she helped him to carry in the dishes. When she saw Khawaja Husain, she immediately recognized him as the captain of the thieves, in spite of his disguise. Looking at him closely, she noticed that he had a dagger hidden under his clothes. 'I am no longer surprised the wretch doesn't want to eat salt with my master,' she said to herself, 'for he is his bitterest enemy and wants to murder him, but I am going to stop him.'

When Marjana had finished serving and letting Abdullah serve, she used the time while they were eating to make the necessary preparations to carry out a most audacious scheme. She had just finished by the time Abdullah came to ask her to serve the fruit, which she then brought and served as soon as Abdullah had cleared the table. Next to Ali Baba she placed a small side table on which she put the wine together with three cups. As she went out, she took Abdullah with her as though they were going to have supper together, leaving Ali Baba, as usual, free to talk, to enjoy the company of his guest and to give him plenty to drink.

It was then that the so-called Khawaja Husain, or rather the captain of the thieves, decided that the moment had come for him to kill Ali Baba. 'I shall get both father and son drunk,' he said to himself, 'and the son, whose life I am willing to spare, won't stop me plunging the dagger into his father's heart. I will then escape through the garden, as I did earlier, before the cook and the slave have finished their supper, or it may be that they will have fallen asleep in the kitchen.'

Instead of having supper, however, Marjana, who had seen through his evil plan, gave him no time to carry out his wicked deed. She put on a dancer's costume, with the proper headdress, and around her waist she tied a belt of gilded silver to which she attached a dagger whose sheath and handle were of the same metal. Finally, she covered her face with a very beautiful mask. Disguised in this manner, she said to Abdullah: 'Abdullah, take your tambourine and let us offer our master's guest and his son's friend the entertainment we sometimes give our master.' Abdullah took the tambourine and began to play as he walked into the room in front of Marjana. Marjana, who followed him, made a deep bow with a deliberate air so as to draw attention to herself, as though asking permission to show what she could do. Seeing that Ali Baba wanted to say something, Abdullah stopped playing his tambourine. 'Come in, Marjana, come in,' said Ali Baba. 'Khawaja Husain will judge what you are capable of and will tell us his opinion. But don't think, sir,' he said, turning to his guest, 'that I have put myself to any expense in offering you this entertainment. I have it in my own home, and as you can see, it is my slave and my cook and housekeeper who provide me with it. I hope you won't find it disagreeable.'

Khawaja Husain, who had not expected Ali Baba to add this entertainment to the supper, was afraid that he would not be able to use the opportunity he thought he had found. But he consoled himself with the hope that, if that happened, another opportunity would arise later if he continued to cultivate the friendship of the father and son. So, although he would have preferred to have done without what was being offered, he still pretended to be grateful, and he courteously indicated that what pleased his host would please him too.

When Abdullah saw that Ali Baba and Khawaja Husain had stopped talking, he began to play his tambourine again and accompanied his playing by singing a dance tune. Marjana, who could dance as well as any professional, performed so admirably that she would have aroused the admiration of any company and not only her present audience, although the so-called Khawaja Husain paid very little attention. After she had danced several dances with the same charm and vigour, she finally drew out the dagger. Holding it in her hand, she then performed a dance in which she surpassed herself with different figures, light movements, astonishing leaps of marvellous energy, now holding the dagger in front, as though to strike, now pretending to plunge it into her own chest. At last, now out of breath, with her left hand she snatched the tambourine from Abdullah and, holding the dagger in her right, she went to present the tambourine to Ali Baba, its bowl uppermost in imitation of the male and female professional dancers who do this to ask for contributions from their spectators.

Ali Baba threw a gold coin into Marjana's tambourine

and, following his father's example, so did his son. Khawaja Husain, seeing she was coming to him too, had already pulled out his purse from his breast to present his offering and was putting his hand out at the very moment that Marjana, with a courage worthy of the firmness and resolve she had shown up till then, plunged the dagger right into his heart and did not pull it out again until he had breathed his last. Terrified by this, Ali Baba and his son both cried out. 'Wretched girl, what have you done?' shouted Ali Baba. 'Do you want to destroy us, my family and myself?' 'I didn't do it to destroy you,' replied Marjana. 'I did it to save you.'

Opening Khawaja Husain's robe, Marjana showed Ali Baba the dagger with which he was armed. 'See what a fine enemy you've been dealing with!' she said. 'Look carefully at his face and you will recognize the bogus oil merchant and the captain of the forty thieves. Remember how he didn't want to eat salt with you – do you need anything more to convince you that he was planning evil? The moment you told me you had such a guest, before I had even seen him I became suspicious. I then set eyes on him and you can see how my suspicions were not unfounded.'

Ali Baba, recognizing the new obligation he was under to Marjana for having saved his life a second time, embraced her and said: 'When I gave you your freedom, I promised you that my gratitude would not stop there but that I would soon add the final touch to my promise. The time has now come and I will make you my daughter-in-law.' Turning to his son, he said: 'I believe you are a dutiful enough son not to find it strange that I am giving you Marjana as a wife without consulting you. You are no less obliged to her than I am. You can see that Khawaja

Husain only made friends with you in order to make it easier for him to murder me treacherously. Had he succeeded, you can be sure that you also would have been sacrificed to his vengeance. Consider, too, that if you take Marjana you will be marrying someone who, as long as we both live, will be the prop and mainstay of my family and yours.' Ali Baba's son, far from showing any displeasure, gave his consent, not only because he did not want to disobey his father but because his own inclinations led in that direction.

Their next concern was to bury the body of the captain by the corpses of the thirty-seven thieves. This was done so secretly that no one knew about it until many years later, when there was no longer any interest in this memorable tale becoming known.

A few days later, Ali Baba celebrated the wedding of his son to Marjana, with a solemn ceremony and a sumptuous banquet which was accompanied by the customary dances, spectacles and entertainments. The friends and neighbours whom he had invited were not told the real reason for the marriage, but they were well acquainted with Marjana's many excellent qualities and Ali Baba had the great satisfaction of finding that they were loud in their praises for his generosity and good-heartedness.

After the wedding, Ali Baba continued to stay away from the cave in the forest. He had not been there since he had taken away the body of his brother, Qasim, together with the gold, which he had loaded on to his three donkeys. This had been out of fear that he would find the thieves there and would fall into their hands. Even after thirty-eight of them, including their captain, had died, he still did not go back, believing that the remaining two, of whose fate he was ignorant, were still alive. But when a year had gone by, seeing that nothing had occurred to cause him any disquiet, he was curious enough to make the trip, taking the necessary precautions to ensure his safety. He mounted his horse and, on approaching the cave, he took it as a good sign that he could see no trace of men or horses. He dismounted, tied up his own horse and, standing in front of the door, he uttered these words – which he had not forgotten: 'Open, Sesame.' The door opened and he entered. The state in which he found everything in the cave led him to conclude that, since around the time when the so-called Khawaja Husain had come to rent a shop in the city, no one had been there and so the band of forty thieves must all since have scattered and been wiped out. He was now certain that he was the only person in the world who knew the secret of how to open the cave and that its treasure was at his disposal. He had a bag with him which he filled with as much gold as his horse could carry, and then returned to the city.

Later he took his son to the cave and taught him the secret of how to enter it and, in time, the two of them passed this on to their descendants. They lived in great splendour, being held in honour as the leading dignitaries in the city. They had profited from their good fortune but used it with restraint.

When she had finished telling this story to King Shahriyar, Shahrazad, seeing it was not yet light, began to recount the story we are now going to hear . . .

Judar and His Brothers

I have also heard that there once was a merchant called
'Umar who left three children, the eldest Salim, the young-
est Judar and the middle one Saliim. He brought them up
until they reached manhood, but his favourite was Judar.
When this was clear to his brothers, they became jealous
of Judar and started to dislike him. Realizing this, their
father, who was then an old man, was afraid that, if he
were to die, they might cause trouble for their brother,
and so he summoned a number of his relations, together
with judicial administrators and men of learning. He told
them to bring out the money and the materials that he
owned, and when they had done this he told them to
divide all this into four parts according to the principles
laid down by Islamic law. When they had made the
division, he gave one portion to each of his sons and kept
one for himself. Then he said: 'This was all my wealth.
Now that I have distributed it, there's no more for them
to have either from me or from each other and so, when
I die, there is no need for them to quarrel. I have given

them their inheritance during my lifetime and the portion that I have kept for myself will go to my wife, their mother, to help with her living expenses.'

Soon after this 'Umar died and, far from being content with what he had done, his other sons wanted to get more from Judar, claiming that it was he who had their father's money. The case was taken to court and the Muslims who had been present at the division of the inheritance gave evidence as to what they knew of it. The judge then kept them from encroaching on each other's share, but the dispute had been costly both for Judar and for his brothers. The latter abandoned their claim for a while, but then schemed against Judar for a second time, and again the case was taken to court, losing them all money. In spite of that they kept on trying to damage Judar, taking the case from one unjust judge to another, losing their own money and wasting his, until all their father's inheritance had been spent on bribery. Judar's brothers then went to their mother and, after jeering at her, they took her money, beat her and drove her away. She went to tell Judar what they had done and began to curse them. 'Don't curse them, mother,' Judar said, 'for God will repay both of them for this. But both they and I are poor, and this wrangling costs money. We have often taken the case before judges, but, far from doing us any good, we have lost all that our father left us and have been disgraced by those who have been called as witnesses. Am I then to have another quarrel with them because of you and take the case to court? This cannot be, so stay here with me and I shall share what food I have with you. Pray for me and God will give both of us our daily bread. Leave them to face God's punishment for what they have done and console yourself with the lines:

If the fool wrongs you, let him be,
And wait awhile for his punishment.
Avoid unhealthy wrongdoing;
A mountain that wrongs another will be ground to
    dust.'

Judar continued to console his mother until she accepted the situation and stayed with him. He then equipped himself with a fishing net and went out every day in a different direction, to the river or the pools or anywhere else where there was water. Some days he would earn ten *nusfs* and on others twenty or thirty. He spent the money on his mother, while at the same time having enough to eat and drink well. His brothers, meanwhile, practised no craft and were unable to trade; they were crushed by poverty and distress, having squandered all that they had taken from their mother, and they became wretched and naked beggars. At times they would approach their mother in all humility, complaining of hunger, and in her tenderness of heart she would give them any food that had gone bad, or if there was anything that had been cooked the day before she would tell them to eat it up quickly and leave before their brother came. 'He wouldn't find this easy to accept,' she would tell them, 'and were he to harden his heart against me, you would disgrace me in his eyes.' They would then wolf down the food and go off.

One day when they came she put out a cooked dish for them, together with some bread, and they began to eat. At that moment, to their mother's shame and confusion, in came their brother, Judar. She hung her head before him, afraid that he might be angry with her, but he smiled at his visitors and welcomed them, exclaiming: 'This is a blessed day! How is it that you have come on such a day to visit me?' He embraced them lovingly and went on: 'I never wanted you to keep away from me and not come here to see me or your mother.' 'By God, brother,' they told him, 'we have been longing for you and we only kept away because we were ashamed of what happened between us, which we bitterly regret. That was the work of the devil, may Almighty God curse him, and you and our mother are our only blessing.' His mother called down blessings on him and praised his generosity, after which he again welcomed his brothers and invited them to stay, saying: 'God is generous and I bring in plenty to live on.' The three were reconciled and Judar's brothers spent the night there sharing his supper and eating breakfast the next day.

He then took his net and left, relying on God, the Provider. His brothers went off and when they came back at noon their mother produced a meal for them, while he himself returned in the evening bringing with him meat and vegetables. Things went on like this for a month, with Judar catching fish, selling them and spending the money he earned on his mother and his brothers, the two of whom doing nothing but eating and amusing themselves. It then happened that one day Judar took his net to the river and made a cast, only to find when he drew it out that it was empty. He made a second cast but again it was empty, and he told himself: 'There are no fish here.' So he went and cast his net somewhere else, but again without success and, although he continued to wander round from one place to another from dawn to dusk, he failed to catch even one single small fish. 'This is strange,' he told himself. 'Are there not any fish in the river any longer and, if so, why?'

With the net over his shoulder he went back sorrowfully and full of care, worried about his brothers and his mother since he had no idea what to give them to eat. He came to a baker's oven around which was a crowd of people with money in their hands wanting to buy bread, while the baker himself was paying no attention to them. He stood there sighing and the baker called out a welcome to him and asked him if he was wanting bread. When he made no reply, the baker said: 'If you don't have the money, take what you need and you can pay me later.' So Judar asked for ten *nusfs'* worth of bread, and the baker gave him an extra ten in cash, telling him to bring him twenty *nusfs'* worth of fish the next day. Judar swore to do that, and he took the bread as well as the money, with which he bought a piece of meat and some vegetables, saying: 'Tomorrow God will help me out of my difficulties.'

When he had gone back home and his mother had cooked the food, he ate his evening meal and went to sleep. The next day he took his net and, when his mother told him to sit down and have his breakfast, he refused, telling her to eat with his brothers. He then went to the river, but after three casts he had to try somewhere else and this went on until the afternoon, by which time he had caught nothing at all. He walked away dispiritedly on a route on which he couldn't avoid passing the baker, and when the baker saw him there, he weighed out the bread and produced the coins, saying: 'Come on, take this and go. If you caught nothing today, you will tomorrow.' Judar wanted to present his excuses, but the baker said: 'Go off; there is no need to explain. If you had caught anything you would have been carrying it with you, and when I saw you empty-handed I realized that you had got nothing. If this happens again tomorrow, don't be ashamed to come for bread, as you can pay me later.'

On the third day he visited the pools until the afternoon, but he found nothing at all there and so he had to return to the baker to fetch the bread and the coins. This went on for seven days, after which he became depressed and made up his mind to go to Lake Qarun. He was on the point of making a cast there when, before he knew it, up rode a Maghribi on a mule. The rider was wearing a splendid robe, and the mule, all of whose trappings were embroidered, carried over its back embroidered saddle-bags. The man dismounted and said: 'Peace be on you, Judar, son of 'Umar,' to which Judar replied: 'And peace be on you, pilgrim.' 'Judar,' said the man, 'there is something I want you to do, and if you do it, it will bring you a great deal of good. You will be my companion and manage my affairs.' Judar asked him what he had in mind, promising to do what he wanted without fail. 'Recite the Fatiha,' the man told him, and when they had both done this, the man brought out a silk cord and told him to tie his hands behind his back as firmly as possible. 'Then throw me into the lake,' he went on, 'and wait a little. If you see my hand raised from the water before the rest of me appears, then throw your net at me and pull me in quickly, but if you see my foot, then leave me, for you will know that I am dead. In that case take the mule and the saddlebags and go to the traders' market, where you will find a Jew called Shumai'a. Give him the mule and he will hand you a hundred dinars. Take them and go on your way, but keep the matter secret.'

Judar tied the man's arms tightly as the man kept telling him to tie the cord tighter, and Judar then did as he was told, throwing him into the lake, where he sank from sight. For a time Judar stayed watching, but then he saw the man's legs coming out of the water. Realizing that he must be dead, he took the mule and went off to the traders' market, where he saw the Jew sitting on a chair in the doorway of his storehouse. At the sight of the mule, the Jew exclaimed: 'He must be dead!', adding: 'And it was his greed that killed him.' He then took the mule from Judar, gave him a hundred dinars and told him to keep the affair secret. Judar went off with the money, after which he got what bread he needed from the baker and gave him a dinar in return. The baker calculated his debt and told him: 'I now owe you two days' worth of bread.' Judar went from the baker to the butcher, to whom he gave another dinar. He took his meat and told the man to credit what was left over from the dinar to his account. Then he fetched vegetables and went home, where he found his brothers pestering his mother for something to eat. She was saying: 'Wait for your brother to come, as I haven't anything here at all.' So he went in and told them to take the food and eat it, at which they fell on the bread like *ghuls*. He gave the rest of the gold to his mother, telling her: 'When my brothers come, give them some money to buy food with while I am away.'

He then spent the night at home, and the next morning, taking his net with him, he went back to Lake Qarun. He was about to make a cast when another Maghribi, even more splendidly equipped than the first, rode up on a mule with a pair of saddlebags and two small boxes, one in each bag. He addressed Judar by name, and when they had exchanged greetings the newcomer asked whether another Maghribi had come on the day before riding a mule like his. Judar was nervous and denied having seen anyone lest he be asked where the man had gone, as if he then said that he had drowned in the lake, the newcomer might accuse him of having been responsible. The man was not taken in by his denial and said: 'Poor fellow, that was my brother, who got here before me.' Judar repeated: 'I don't know anything about this,' but the man went on: 'Didn't you tie him up and throw him into the lake, after he had told you that if his hands appeared you were to throw your net and pull him out quickly but that if his feet came up he would be dead? In that case you were to take his mule to the Jew, Shumai'a, who would give you a hundred dinars. It was his feet that appeared and you did take the mule to the Jew, who did give you the money.' 'If you know all that, why do you ask?' said Judar, and the man replied: 'Because I want you to do the same thing to me as you did to my brother.' He then produced a silk cord and said: 'Tie me up and throw me in. If what happened to my brother happens to me, take the mule to the Jew and get a hundred dinars from him. Come on now.' Judar went forward and, having tied him up, he gave him a push so that he fell into the lake and sank. When Judar had waited for some time, he saw the man's feet emerging from the water and he exclaimed: 'He has died miserably! God willing, Maghribis will come to me every day to be tied up and die, and if I get a hundred dinars for each dead man, that will be enough for me.'

He then went off with the mule, and on seeing him the Jew said: 'The other one must be dead.' 'Long life to you,' replied Judar, and the Jew repeated: 'This is the reward of the greedy,' after which he took the mule and gave Judar a hundred dinars. Judar went off with the money to give to his mother, who asked where he had got it. When he told her, she said: 'You shouldn't go to Lake Qarun again, as I'm afraid that you may come to some harm at the hands of these Maghribis.' 'Mother,' he told her, 'I only throw them into the water because they want me to.

What am I supposed to do? This business brings me in a hundred dinars a day and I come home quickly. By God, I'm not going to stop going to the lake until there are no more Maghribis to be seen.'

On the third day he went off and, as he was standing there, another Maghribi appeared riding on a mule with saddlebags, even more splendidly equipped than the first two. He greeted Judar by name, causing him to wonder to himself how they all came to know him, and when he had returned the greeting, the man asked him whether any Maghribis had passed by that spot. 'Yes, two,' he said, and the man then asked where they had gone. 'I tied them up and threw them into this lake, where they drowned,' Judar told him, adding: 'And this is what will happen to you too.' The man laughed and said: 'Poor fellow, every living creature meets its destined fate,' after which he dismounted from his mule and, producing the silken cord, he told Judar to do the same thing with him as he had done with the others. 'Put your hands behind your back so that I can tie them, for I am in a hurry and time is passing,' said Judar. The man did this and Judar tied him up and gave him a push so that he fell into the lake. He then stood waiting and this time the Maghribi raised his hands out of the water and called to him to throw his net. Judar did this and when he had pulled the man in, he discovered that he was clutching two fish coloured like red coral, one in each hand. 'Open the boxes,' the man told him, and when this had been done, he put one fish in each of them and then closed them up. He then embraced Judar and kissed him on both cheeks, saying: 'May God rescue you from every hardship. Had you not thrown me the net and pulled me out, I would have gone on holding these fish and stayed submerged until I died,

for I should not have been able to get out of the water.'
'For God's sake, pilgrim,' Judar said, 'tell me about the
two who drowned earlier and about these two fish as well
as about the Jew.' THE MAGHRIBI REPLIED:

You must know, Judar, that both of them were my
brothers; one of them was called 'Abd al-Salam and the
other 'Abd al-Ahad, while my name is 'Abd al-Samad. The
'Jew' is another of our brothers; his name is 'Abd al-Rahim
and far from being a Jew, he is a Maliki Muslim.* Our
father taught us magic, as well as how to solve riddles and
to uncover hidden treasures. We four brothers practised
our magic craft until the *marids* and the *'ifrits* became our
servants. Then when our father, whose name was 'Abd
al-Wadud, died he left us a great inheritance and we
divided up the treasures, the wealth and the talismans
until we came to the books. We began to share them out
but we could not agree on one of them, a book called
Legends of the Ancients, a unique and invaluable work,
worth more than its weight in jewels, as it contained an
account of all hidden treasures together with the solutions
to riddles. Our father had used it in his work; we ourselves
knew a small section of it by heart and each of us wanted
to own it in order to discover what else was there.

When we began to argue about it, we were joined by
our father's teacher, who had instructed him and taught
him magic and divination, a man called al-Abtan the seer.
He told us to fetch him the book, and when we had given
it to him he said: 'You are the sons of my son and I cannot
wrong any one of you. Whichever of you wants to get
this book must go on a quest for the treasure of al-

---

* Reference to Malik ibn Anas, founder of one of the principal schools
of Islamic law.

Shamardal and fetch me his celestial globe, his kohl case, the signet ring and the sword. A *marid* named al-Ra'd al-Qasif serves the ring, and no king or sultan has any power over its owner, so that if he wants to rule the whole wide world, that will be within his power. As for the sword, if its bearer draws it in the face of an army and brandishes it, the army will be routed, while if, as he is brandishing it, he says: "Kill this army," a bolt of fire will come from the sword and destroy it all. Whoever has the globe can, if he wants, sit inspecting all lands from east to west and whatever part he wants to see, he can do so by turning the globe where he wants and looking into it. He will then have a view of the land and its people as though they were all there in front of him. If he is angry with any city and turns the globe towards the sun with the intention of burning the city to the ground, this is what will happen. As for the kohl case, whoever uses its contents on his eyelids will see all the treasures of the earth.'

Al-Abtan continued: 'I lay down one condition on you: whoever proves unable to open up this treasure will have no right to the book, while whoever succeeds in bringing me the four treasures will be its rightful owner.' When we had agreed to the condition, he went on: 'Know, my children, that the treasure of al-Shamardal is under the control of the sons of the Red King. Your father told me that he had tried to uncover it but had failed, and the Red King's sons had fled from him to an Egyptian lake, known as the lake of Qarun, where they defied him. He followed them to Egypt but was unable to overcome them because the lake into which they had entered was guarded by a talisman. After this failure, your father came and complained to me, and I cast a horoscope for him which showed me that the only person who could take the treasure was a young Cairene by the name of Judar, son of 'Umar, through whom the sons of the Red King could be captured. This Judar was a fisherman, and the place to meet him was by Lake Qarun. The talismanic spell could only be broken if Judar were to tie the hands of whoever was destined to succeed and then throw him into the lake. There the treasure seeker would have to fight with the Red King's sons; if he was the lucky one, he would manage to seize them, but if not, he would die and his feet would emerge, while in the case of the successful man it would be his hands. Judar would then need to throw him the net and bring him out of the water.' My brothers said: 'We will go even if this means our death.' I said that I would go too, but our brother, the 'Jew', told us that he wanted no part of this, and we arranged that he would go to Cairo disguised as a Jewish merchant. If any one of us drowned in the lake, he was to take the mule and the saddlebags from Judar and give him a hundred dinars. The first of us to come to you was killed by the sons of the Red King and they went on to kill my second brother, but they could not get the better of me and so I seized them.

'Where are they, then?' Judar asked. 'You saw them, didn't you?' the man said. 'I shut them up in the two boxes.' 'But those were fish,' objected Judar. 'No, they weren't,' replied the man. 'They were *'ifrits* in the shape of fish. But you must know,' he went on, 'that it is you and you alone who can open up the treasure. Are you willing to follow my instructions and to go with me to Fes and Meknes, where we can do this? I will give you whatever you want and I swear that you will be a brother to me in the sight of God. Afterwards you will be able to go back to your family with a happy heart.' 'Pilgrim,' replied Judar, 'I am responsible for my mother and my two brothers. It is I who provides for them, and if I go off with you, who will give them their daily bread?' 'That is a feeble excuse,' the man replied, 'for, if it is a matter of expense, we'll give you a thousand dinars to pass on to your mother to spend until you get back home, and if you go, you will be back within four months.' When Judar heard him say 'a thousand dinars', he told him: 'Produce the money, pilgrim, and I will leave it with my mother and go off with you.' So the man brought it out for him, and on taking it off to his mother, Judar told her of his encounter with the Maghribi. 'Take these dinars,' he said, 'and spend them on yourself and on my brothers, for I am going to the west with the Maghribi. I shall be away for four months and I shall do very well for myself, so pray for me, mother.' 'You will make me lonely, my son,' she told him, 'and I am afraid for you.' 'No harm can come to one whom God protects, and the Maghribi is a good man,' he told her, and he went on to tell her how lucky he was. She said: 'May God soften his heart towards you. Go with the man, my son, and perhaps he will give you something.' So he said goodbye to her and left.

When he got back, 'Abd al-Samad, the Maghribi, asked him whether he had consulted his mother. 'Yes,' he replied, 'and she blessed me.' 'Get up behind me,' 'Abd al-Samad told him, and when he had mounted on the mule's back the two of them travelled on from noon until the time of the afternoon prayer. By then Judar was hungry, but he could not see that 'Abd al-Samad had anything to eat with him and so he said: 'I wonder, pilgrim, whether you have forgotten to bring any food with you to eat on the way.' 'Are you hungry?' the man asked, and when Judar said that he was, he dismounted together with

Judar and said: 'Bring down the saddlebags.' When Judar had done this, 'Abd al-Samad asked him: 'What would you like, my brother?' 'Whatever there is,' replied Judar, but 'Abd al-Samad insisted that he say what he wanted. 'Bread and cheese,' Judar told him. 'Poor fellow,' replied 'Abd al-Samad, 'that's not for the likes of you. Ask for something good.' 'Just at the moment anything would be good,' said Judar. 'Do you like roast chicken?' he was asked, and when he had said yes, 'Abd al-Samad asked whether he liked rice with honey. After he had again said yes, 'Abd al-Samad went on to ask about a string of different dishes, until he had named twenty-four of them. Judar said to himself: 'He must be mad. How can he produce these for me when he has neither kitchen nor cook? I'd better tell him that that's enough.' So he said: 'Enough of that. Are you trying to make me long for all these dishes when I can't see anything at all?' 'You are welcome, Judar,' replied 'Abd al-Samad, and he then put his hand in the saddlebag and brought out a gold plate on which were two hot roast chickens. He put his hand in again and this time he took out another gold plate with a kebab on it, and went on drawing plates from the saddlebag until, to Judar's astonishment, he had produced every single one of the twenty-four types of food that he had mentioned. 'Eat, you poor fellow,' said 'Abd al-Samad. 'Sir,' answered Judar, 'have you put a kitchen and people to cook for you in the saddlebag?' 'Abd al-Samad laughed and said: 'It has a talismanic charm whose servant, if asked, would immediately produce a thousand different types of food every hour.' 'What a good bag it is!' exclaimed Judar.

The two companions then ate their fill, after which 'Abd al-Samad threw away the leftovers and put the empty dishes back in the saddlebag. He reached into it again and drew out a jug from which they drank and which they used for their ablutions before performing the afternoon prayer. 'Abd al-Samad then returned it to the bag, into which he also put the two boxes. He loaded the saddlebags on to the mule, mounted and told Judar to get up as well, so that they could set off. He asked Judar if he knew how far they had come from Cairo and when Judar said: 'By God, I don't,' he told him: 'We have covered the distance of a month's journey.' 'How can that be?' Judar asked, and 'Abd al-Samad explained: 'The mule that we are riding is a *marid* of the *jinn*, which can cover a year's journey in a single day, but for your sake it is going slowly.'

When the two had mounted, they set off westwards. In the evening 'Abd al-Samad brought out supper from the saddlebags, and in the morning, breakfast. For four days they went on like this, riding until midnight and then dismounting to sleep, before setting off again in the morning, with Judar asking 'Abd al-Samad for anything he wanted and 'Abd al-Samad producing it for him from the saddlebags. On the fifth day they arrived at Fes and Meknes, and when they entered the city everyone who met 'Abd al-Samad greeted him and kissed his hand. That went on until they came to a door on which he knocked. It opened to show a girl radiant as the moon, to whom he said: 'Rahma, my daughter, open up the pavilion for us.' 'Willingly, father,' she replied, and she went back in, swaying her hips in a way that robbed Judar of his wits, making him say to himself that she must be a king's daughter. She opened the door of the pavilion and 'Abd al-Samad took the saddlebags from the mule's back and said to it: 'Go off now, God bless you.' At that a chasm opened into which the mule went down before the earth closed up again. 'Sheltering God,' exclaimed Judar, 'praise be to You for allowing us to escape from the back of that mule!' 'Don't be surprised, Judar,' 'Abd al-Samad said. 'I told you that this was an '*ifrit*. Now, come into the pavilion with me.'

They both went in and Judar was astonished at the quantity of splendid furnishings, the rarities, the strings of jewels and the precious stones that he saw there. When they were seated, 'Abd al-Samad said to his daughter: 'Rahma, fetch such-and-such a package.' She got up and brought a package which she put down in front of her father and, when he had opened it, he drew out of it a robe worth a thousand dinars. 'Put this on, Judar, for you are welcome here,' he said. Judar did so and it made him look as though he was one of the kings of the west. 'Abd al-Samad then put his hand into the saddlebags, which he had placed in front of him, and took out plates containing foods of various sorts until he had produced a meal with forty different dishes. 'Come up and eat,' he told Judar, 'and don't blame me, for I don't know what food you would like, but if you tell me, I shall get it for you without delay.' 'By God, sir pilgrim,' Judar replied, 'I am fond of all kinds of foods and there is nothing that I dislike. You don't need to ask me questions; just bring everything that you can think of and I shall do nothing but eat.'

Judar stayed with 'Abd al-Samad for twenty days, on each of which he was given a robe, and food was produced from the saddlebags. 'Abd al-Samad never bought any meat or bread and never cooked, as he took all that he needed from the saddlebags, including various kinds of fruits. Then, on the twenty-first day, he told Judar to come with him, saying that this was the day on which the treasure of al-Shamardal was destined to be opened. Judar left with him and the two of them walked through the city and then out of it, where they each mounted a mule and travelled on until noon. They came to a river where 'Abd al-Samad dismounted, and Judar followed his instructions to do the same. 'Abd al-Samad called to two slaves and gestured to them with his hand, at which they took the mules, each going off on his way, but after a brief absence one of them came back with a tent which he set up, while the other brought a mattress which he laid down in the tent, surrounding it with pillows and cushions. One of them then fetched the two boxes containing the fish, while the other brought the saddlebags. 'Come here, Judar,' said 'Abd al-Samad, and when Judar had come and sat down beside him, 'Abd al-Samad brought out plates of food from the saddlebags and they ate their morning meal. Then 'Abd al-Samad took the boxes and recited a spell over them. 'Here we are, sorcerer of the world, have mercy on us,' came two voices from within, and while they were calling for help and 'Abd al-Samad was reciting his spell, the two boxes burst into pieces. As the pieces flew apart, two bound figures appeared, saying: 'Spare us, sorcerer of the world. What are you going to do with us?' 'I am going to burn you to death unless you pledge to help me open the treasure of al-Shamardal,' 'Abd al-Samad replied. 'We give you our pledge and we shall do this for you, but on condition that you fetch Judar, the fisherman, as it is only he who can succeed in opening it, and he alone can enter the treasure chamber.' 'I have already brought him, and he is here, listening to you and looking at you.'

When the two had given 'Abd al-Samad their word to perform the task, he set them free. Then he brought out a wand and some tablets of red carnelian which he placed on top of the wand. He took a brazier in which he placed charcoal, and with a single puff he lit it, before fetching incense. 'Judar,' he said, 'I am going to recite a spell and put the incense on the fire. When I start my spell, I shall not be able to say anything else lest it be broken, so I want to tell you what you must do in order to reach your goal.' 'Tell me, then,' said Judar, and 'Abd al-Samad continued: 'You have to know that when I recite my spell and put the incense on the fire, the water in the river will dry up and you will see a golden door, as big as the gate of a city, with two metal rings. Go down to it, knock on it gently and then wait for a while before knocking again more loudly. Wait again, and then give three knocks, one after the other. You will hear a voice saying: "Who is knocking on the door of the treasure house without knowing how to unravel its mysteries?" You are then to say: "I am Judar, the fisherman, son of 'Umar." The door will open and out will come someone with a sword in his hand and he will say: "If you are that man, stretch out your neck and I shall cut off your head." Do that without fear, for when he lifts the sword up in his hand and strikes you, he will collapse in front of you; you will see him as a lifeless figure and his blow will neither hurt you nor do you any harm, whereas if you disobey him, he will kill you. When by obeying him you have destroyed his talismanic power, go in and knock on another door that you will see there. This time a rider will come out mounted on a horse with a spear carried over his shoulder. He will say: "What has brought you to this place which neither man nor *jinn* can enter?" When he then brandishes his spear at you, expose your breast to him and he will strike you before collapsing on the spot as a lifeless body. If you don't do this, he will kill you. Enter the third door and a man will come out to meet you holding a bow and arrows. He will shoot at you and you must expose your breast to him, so that he falls lifeless before you; if you do not, you will be killed. Then go and knock on the fourth door. It will be opened for you and an enormous lion will come out and attack you, opening its mouth to show that it wants to eat you. Don't be afraid and don't run away, but when it reaches you, hold out your hand to it and it will instantly fall down, having done you no harm. On entering the fifth door, you will be met by a black slave who will ask you who you are. When you tell him that you are Judar, he will say: "If that is so, then open the sixth door." Go up to it and say: "'Isa, tell Musa to open the door," at which it will open. Go through and you will find two snakes, one on the left and the other on the right. Both of them will open their mouths and attack you instantly. You are to hold out your hands to them and each of them will bite a hand, but if you don't do that, they will kill you. When you go in to knock on the seventh door, your mother will come out and say: "Welcome, my son. Come forward so that I may greet you." Say to her: "Stay away from me and take off your clothes." "My son," she will answer, "I am your mother to whom you owe a debt for having suckled and raised you. How can you make me strip?" You must threaten to kill her if she refuses, and if you look to your right you will find a sword hanging on the wall. Take it and draw it against her, ordering her to take off her clothes. She will try to delude you, humbling herself before you, but have no pity on her and every time that she takes something off, tell her to remove the rest. Keep on threatening to kill her until she has taken off all her clothes, after which she will collapse.

'You will then have unravelled all the mysteries and broken the talismanic spells, so saving your own life.

When you enter the treasure chamber, you will find gold lying in heaps, but pay no attention to any of it. At the upper end of the chamber, you will see a recessed room screened by a curtain. Pull aside the curtain and there you will find al-Shamardal, the magician, lying on a golden couch, with, by his head, something round that gleams like the moon. This is the celestial globe; he himself is girt with a sword, and on his finger is a ring and round his neck a chain to which is attached a kohl case. Fetch these four treasures and take care not to forget anything that I have told you or to disobey the instructions, for if you do you will have cause for regret and find yourself in fearful danger.'

'Abd al-Samad repeated these instructions a second time and then a third and a fourth, until Judar said: 'I know them by heart, but how can anyone face these talismans that you have mentioned or endure such fearful horrors?' 'Don't be afraid, Judar,' 'Abd al-Samad replied, 'these are nothing but lifeless figures,' and he set about calming Judar's fears until Judar exclaimed: 'I rely on God!' After that, 'Abd al-Samad threw the incense on the fire and started to recite a spell. This went on for some time until the water disappeared and the bed of the river could be seen, showing the door of the treasure chamber. Judar went down and knocked, after which he heard a voice saying: 'Who is knocking on the door of the treasure house without knowing how to unravel its mysteries?' When Judar gave his name, the door opened and out to meet him came a figure with a drawn sword, who told him to stretch out his neck. When he did so, the figure struck him and then collapsed. The same thing happened at the second door and this went on until he had put the talismans of all seven doors out of action.

Then his mother came out and greeted him, but he replied: 'What are you?' She said: 'I am your mother, to whom you owe a debt because I suckled and raised you, and I carried you for nine months, my son.' He told her to take off her clothes, but she protested: 'You are my son. How can you strip me?' 'Take them off,' he repeated, 'or else I shall behead you with this sword,' and, stretching out his hand, he unsheathed it against her, saying: 'Unless you strip off your clothes, I shall kill you.' After a long wrangle she yielded to his repeated threats and took off some, but he insisted that she take off the rest, and after another wrangle she took off something else. This went on and she kept exclaiming: 'My son, your upbringing has been wasted!' until only her drawers were left. 'Have you a heart of stone, my son,' she protested, 'that you would shame me by uncovering my private parts? This is unlawful.' 'That is true,' he said, 'so don't take off your drawers.' At that she gave a cry and called out: 'He has made a mistake, so beat him!' and the servants of the treasure gathered together and rained blows like raindrops on him, giving him a beating which he was never to forget in his life. Then they pushed him away and threw him outside the gate of the treasure chamber, whose doors closed shut as they had been before.

'Abd al-Samad picked him up immediately as the river started to flow again. He recited a spell over Judar until he came back to his senses and recovered from his stupor. 'What have you done, poor fellow?' 'Abd al-Samad asked, and Judar told him: 'I overcame all the obstacles until I came to my mother. We had a long wrangle and she started taking off her clothes, until, when only her drawers were left, she said: "Don't put me to shame, for it would be unlawful to uncover my private parts." So out of pity for her I let her keep them on, at which she shouted out: "He has made a mistake; beat him!" Then people came from I don't know where and beat me almost to death, after which they pushed me out. I don't know what happened to me after that.' 'Did I not forbid you to disobey the instructions?' asked 'Abd al-Samad, adding: 'You have injured me and injured yourself, for had she stripped off her drawers, we should have got what we wanted. As it is, you will have to stay with me until this same day next year.'

He immediately summoned his two slaves, who took down the tent and carried it off, coming back after a short absence with the two mules. 'Abd al-Samad and Judar each mounted one of them and then returned to Fes. Judar stayed with 'Abd al-Samad enjoying good food and drink, with splendid clothes being given to him every day, until the year had passed and the appointed day had come again. 'Abd al-Samad told him of this and said: 'Come with me.' Judar agreed and was then taken outside the city, where the two of them saw the two slaves with the two mules. They mounted and rode to the river, where the slaves pitched the tent and equipped it with its furnishings. When 'Abd al-Samad had brought out the saddlebags, they ate their morning meal and then, as before, he produced the wand and the tablets, lit the fire and fetched the incense. 'Judar,' he said, 'I want to give you your instructions.' 'Sir pilgrim,' Judar replied, 'if I had forgotten the beating that I got, then I would have forgotten the instructions too.' 'You remember them, then?' 'Abd al-Samad asked, and when Judar said that he did, 'Abd al-Samad went on: 'Look after yourself and don't think that the woman is your mother. She is only a talismanic figure shaped like your mother, whose purpose is to get you to make a mistake. You may have escaped alive the first time, but if you get it wrong this time, what they throw out will be your dead body.' 'If I do get it wrong,' said Judar, 'then I shall deserve to be burned.'

So 'Abd al-Samad put the incense on the fire and recited his spell, at which the river dried up. Judar went and knocked on the door and, after it had opened, he disabled the seven talismans before reaching his 'mother', who greeted him as her son. 'How can I be your son, you damned creature? Take off your clothes,' he said. She began to try to trick him, removing one garment after another until only her drawers were left. 'Take them off, damn you,' he said, and when she had done so she was only a lifeless form.

He entered the treasure chamber but paid no attention to the gold that he saw lying in heaps. Instead, he went to the recess where he saw al-Shamardal, the magician, lying girt with his sword and with a ring on his finger, the kohl case on his breast and above his head the celestial globe. Judar went up to him, unfastened the sword and took the ring, the globe and the kohl case. As he went out, a fanfare sounded as the servants of the treasure called out to congratulate him on the gift that he had been given. This fanfare continued until he had left the chamber and returned to 'Abd al-Samad, who, for his part, stopped reciting his spell and burning the incense, and got up to greet him and embrace him, before taking the four treasures that were now handed to him. He then called to the slaves, who took the tent away and came back with the mules, on which 'Abd al-Samad and Judar rode back to Fes. 'Abd al-Samad then brought out the saddlebags and began taking plates laid with various types of food from them, until a whole meal was set out before him. 'Eat,

Judar, my brother,' he said, and when Judar had eaten his fill, the leftovers were emptied out on to other plates and the empty ones were put back in the saddlebag.

'Abd al-Samad now said: 'Judar, you have left your land and your own country for my sake and you have done what I wanted you to do for me. I now owe you a wish, so wish for whatever you want. It is Almighty God Who grants it and I am merely the means towards this. Do not be ashamed to ask for what you want, for you deserve it.' 'Sir,' replied Judar, 'the wish that I would make to God and then to you is that you would give me this pair of saddlebags.' 'Fetch them,' said 'Abd al-Samad, and when they had been brought, he said: 'Take them, for you have a right to them and if you had asked for something different I would have given it to you. But, poor man, they will only help you when it comes to food. You have faced hardships with me, and I promised to send you home with a happy heart, so in addition to these bags from which you can get your food, I will give you another pair filled with gold and jewels. I shall see that you get back to your own country, where you can become a merchant and clothe yourself and your family without concerning yourself about expense, taking your food and that of your family from the saddlebags. The way to use them is to put your hand in one with the words: "I conjure you by the great names to whom you owe obedience, servant of the saddlebag, to produce me such-and-such a dish." Even if you asked for a thousand different ones each day, they would be brought for you.'

'Abd al-Samad then summoned a slave with a mule, and filled one saddlebag with gold and another with jewels and precious stones. 'Mount on this mule,' he said to Judar, 'and the slave will walk on before you until he brings you to the door of your own house, because he knows the way. When you get there, take the saddlebags but hand the mule over to the slave, who will bring it back. Do not let anyone know your secret, and now I entrust you to God.' 'May He reward you amply,' replied Judar, and he then put the saddlebags on the mule's back and mounted, as the slave walked on in front of him. The mule followed the slave that day and all through the night until morning on the second day, when Judar entered by the Bab al-Nasr, only to discover his mother sitting there as a beggar. In consternation he dismounted and threw himself on her. She burst into tears at the sight of him, and he mounted her on the mule and walked by her stirrup until he got home. There he helped her to dismount and, taking the saddlebags, he left the mule in the charge of the slave, who took it and went back to his master, for both slave and mule were devils.

As for Judar himself, he found it hard to bear that his mother had been reduced to begging and when he had got to the house he asked her whether his brothers were well. When she told him that they were, he asked her why she had been begging on the street. 'Because I was hungry,' she replied. 'Before I left I gave you a hundred dinars one day, a hundred on the next and a thousand on the day I went,' he said. 'My son,' she replied, 'your two brothers cheated me and took the money, saying that they wanted to buy goods with it, but when they got it they drove me away and I have been so hungry that I had to start begging in the streets.' 'Mother,' he told her, 'now that I am back, no harm will come to you and you need never have any worries, for this pair of saddlebags is full of gold and jewels, as well as many other good things.' 'You are a lucky man, my son,' she told him. 'May God be pleased with you and grant you more of His favours. But go and bring me some bread, because I had nothing to eat yesterday evening and am perishing of hunger.' 'You are very welcome to this, mother,' Judar said, laughing. 'Ask for whatever you want to eat and I shall bring it for you immediately, for I've no need to buy anything from the market or to find a cook.' 'You don't seem to have anything with you, my son,' she objected, but he said: 'In these saddlebags are all kinds of foods.' 'Anything that one has is enough to satisfy hunger,' she said. 'That is right,' he replied, 'and when there are no provisions, a man can be satisfied with the minimum, but when that's not the case, he will want to eat well. I now have the means, so ask for what you want.' She asked for hot bread and a bit of cheese, but he objected: 'This does not suit your status.' 'You know my status, so give me what fits it,' she said, and he told her: 'What is suitable is roast meat, roast chicken, rice with pepper, sausages, stuffed gourds, stuffed lamb, stuffed ribs and sugared vermicelli with broken nuts and honey, together with fried doughnuts and almond pastry.' She thought that he was laughing at her and making fun of her, and so she called out in disgust: 'What's happened to you? Are you dreaming or mad?' 'What makes you think that I am mad?' he asked, and she replied: 'Because you mention all these splendid dishes, and who could afford to pay for them or know how to cook them?' 'I swear by my life,' he said, 'that I will certainly give you every one of them to eat this very minute.' 'I don't see anything,' she objected. On his instructions she brought the saddlebags, but when she felt them, she found them empty. However, she passed them to him and after he had stretched out his hand, he produced dishes laden with food until every single thing that he had mentioned was there. 'The bags are small,' his mother said, 'and there was nothing in them and yet you have taken all this out of them. Where were these dishes?' He told her: 'You must know, mother, that the Maghribi gave these bags to me. They have a talismanic spell and the talisman has a servant. Whoever wants something must recite the magic names and say: "Servant of the saddlebag, bring me such-and-such a type of food," and he will then fetch it.' 'May I reach in and ask for something?' she asked, and when he had agreed to this, she stretched out her hand and said: 'I conjure you, servant of the saddlebag, by the duty you owe to these names, to bring me stuffed ribs.' She then saw that there was a plate in the bag and, when she reached in and took it, she found that on it were expensive stuffed ribs. So she went on to ask for bread and for every type of food that she wanted, after which Judar told her: 'When you have finished eating, mother, put what is left of the food on to other plates and put the empty ones back in the bag, for this is how the talisman works. Look after the bag.'

Judar's mother then took the bag into her own keeping, and he told her to keep the secret and to carry the bag with her. 'Whenever you need something,' he went on, 'take it from the bag. Use it for alms-giving and for feeding my brothers whether I am there or not.' He and she then began to eat and at that point in came the two brothers, who had heard the news from one of the locals. This man had said: 'Your brother has come back, riding on a mule, with a slave going ahead of him, wearing a most magnificent robe.' They each said to the other: 'I wish that we had not mistreated our mother, for she is bound to tell him what we did and we shall be put to shame.' But then one of them said: 'She has a soft heart, and even if she does tell him, his heart is even softer than hers and he will accept our excuses.' So they went in to meet him and he rose to his feet and greeted them warmly before telling them to sit down and eat, which they did as they were weak with hunger. They went on until they were full, and Judar then told them to take what was left of the food and distribute it to the poor and needy. 'Brother,' they said, 'leave it for our supper.' 'When it is time for supper, you can have even more than this,' promised Judar, and so they took out the leftovers and told every poor man that passed them: 'Take and eat,' until there was nothing left. They then took back the plates, and Judar told his mother to put them into the saddlebag.

That evening, Judar entered the courtyard and produced a meal with forty different dishes from the bag, after which he went out and sat between his brothers, telling his mother to bring in the supper. She came and when she saw the plates filled with food, she set the table and brought in the plates one after the other until all forty were there. They all had their supper and Judar again told his brothers to take what was left of the food and to distribute it among the poor and needy, which they did. After supper he brought them sweetmeats, which they ate, with the leftovers, on his instructions, being given to the neighbours. The same thing happened the next day at breakfast, and things went on like this for ten days. Then one of the brothers said to the other: 'How does this come about? Our brother produces a guest meal for us in the morning, another at noon, a third in the evening, and sweetmeats late at night, and he distributes what is left over to the poor. This is the kind of thing that sultans do, and how has he become so prosperous? Should you not ask about all these different kinds of foods and the sweetmeats, as well as about the leftovers he distributes to the poor? We never see him buying anything or lighting a fire, and he has neither kitchen nor cook.' 'By God, I don't know the answer to that,' replied his brother, 'but do you know anyone who will tell us the real secret behind it?' 'The only one who could do that is our mother,' said the other.

So they made a plan and went to her while Judar was absent, telling her that they were hungry. She said that she had good news for them and then went to the court-yard, where she made her request to the servant of the saddlebags and produced a hot meal. 'This food is hot,' they said, 'but you neither cooked nor lit a fire.' 'The dishes came from the saddlebags,' she told them, and when they asked what the bags really were, she told them that they were covered by a talismanic spell and had to be asked for from the servant of the talisman. She then told them the story of the bags, but warned them to keep it a secret. 'The secret is safe with us, mother,' they assured her, 'but tell us how it works.' So she taught them, and they started to stretch out their hands and bring out whatever they wanted, without Judar knowing anything about it.

When they had learned how to use the saddlebags, Salim said to Saliim: 'Brother, how long are we going to be like Judar's slaves, living off his bounty? Why shouldn't we play some trick on him and get the saddlebags for ourselves?' 'How can we do that?' asked Saliim, and his brother said: 'We can sell him to the captain of the Suez fleet.' 'But how can we arrange to sell him?' the other asked. 'You and I will go to the captain and invite him to a meal, together with two of his men. Whatever I tell Judar you are to confirm it, and at the end of the evening

I'll show you what I shall do.' After they had agreed on this, the two of them went to the captain's house and told him: 'Captain, we have come on an errand which will please you.' 'Good,' replied the captain, and they went on: 'We two are brothers and we have a third one, a debauched good-for-nothing. When our father died he left us some money, which we divided up, and our brother took his share of the inheritance, only to spend it on depravity and evil living. When he had been reduced to poverty, he got the better of us, complaining to the police that we had taken his money and the money of our father. We took the affair up to the courts but lost money, and then, after he had left us alone for a time, he lodged a second complaint. This went on until we had been impoverished, but he has not stopped persecuting us, so causing us great distress, and what we want is for you to buy him from us.' The captain said: 'If you can bring him here to me by some means or other, I shall quickly send him off to sea.' 'We cannot bring him,' they replied, 'but you can come as our guest and bring with you two of your men and no more. Then, when he falls asleep, all five of us, working together, can seize him and gag him and you can take him off from the house under cover of night and do what you want with him.' 'To hear is to obey,' the captain said, adding: 'Will you sell him for forty dinars?' They agreed to this and told him to come to such-and-such a quarter after the evening prayer, where he would find one of them waiting for him.

He told them to go off, and they went to look for Judar. After having waited for some time, Salim went up to him and kissed his hand. Then, when Judar asked him what he wanted, Salim said: 'You must know, brother, that I have a friend who often invited me to his house while you were away. He showed me innumerable kindnesses and always treated me hospitably, as my brother knows. I greeted him today and he invited me to a meal, but I told him that I couldn't leave my brother, at which he said: "Bring him, too." I told him: "He won't agree to that, but perhaps you and your brothers" – who were sitting with him – "would come to us as guests?" I gave the invitation thinking that they would refuse, but in fact they accepted it and my friend told me to wait for him at the door of the small mosque, where he would come with his brothers. I'm afraid that he will arrive, and although I'm ashamed to press you, would you set my mind at ease by entertaining them tonight, for you are so generous a person? If you don't want to do this, let me take them to a neighbour's house.' 'Why should you do that?' asked Judar. 'Is our own house too small or have we no food to give them? Shame on you for having consulted me. All you need is enough good food and more for them, as well as sweetmeats, and if you bring in guests while I am away, then ask our mother to produce extra food for you. So off you go and fetch them, for this will bring us blessings.'

Salim now kissed Judar's hand and went to sit down by the mosque door where he waited until after the evening prayer, when he saw the captain and his men approaching. He took them into the house, where Judar greeted them, sat them down and chatted with them, not knowing what their secret purpose was. He then told his mother to serve supper, and she fetched whatever he asked for from the saddlebag, until forty different dishes had been set before the visitors. They ate until they had had enough and the meal was then cleared away, a meal which the sailors thought they owed to Salim's generosity. When the first third of the night had passed, Judar produced sweetmeats for them, which were served by Salim, while Judar and Saliim stayed seated. The conspirators then said that they wanted to sleep, so Judar got up and went off to sleep himself, while the others dozed until they could take him unawares. Then they got up and made a concerted attack on him, and before he knew what was happening, he was gagged and bound. They carried him out of the house under cover of night, and then sent him off to Suez, where his feet were chained. He remained silent and stayed there toiling like a prisoner or a slave for a whole year.

So much for him, but as for his brothers, when morning came they went to their mother and told her that he was not yet awake. 'Wake him up, then,' their mother said to them. 'Where was he sleeping?' they asked. 'With the guests,' she told them, and they said: 'Perhaps he went off with them, while we were asleep. He has tasted the pleasures of life in foreign parts and has a wish to make his way into treasure chambers. We heard him talking with the Maghribis, and they were telling him that they would take him with them and uncover a treasure for him.' 'Did he meet with Maghribis?' their mother asked, and when they told her that that was who their guests had been, she agreed that he might have gone with them, adding: 'But God will guide him on his way, for he is a lucky man and will meet with great good fortune.' Then she burst into tears, as she found it hard to part from him, but the brothers said: 'You damned woman, are you so fond of Judar, while as for us, you would be neither glad nor sorry if we were here or not? Aren't we your sons, just as Judar is your son?' 'You are,' she told them, 'but you are a pair of wretches who have never helped me in any way or done any good to me since the day of your father's death, while as for Judar, he has been more than good to me, comforting me and being generous to me. It is only right that I should weep for him because of the help that he has given both to me and to the two of you.'

When the brothers heard what their mother had to say, they showered abuse on her and beat her, after which they went in and searched through the saddlebags, removing the jewels from one and gold from the other, as well as taking the pair covered by the talismanic spell. 'This was our father's money,' they told their mother. 'No, by God,' she replied. 'It belongs to your brother, Judar, and he brought it from the Maghrib.' 'That's a lie,' they insisted. 'It belonged to our father and we have a right to dispose of it.' So they divided it between themselves, but they then quarrelled over the talismanic saddlebags, each saying that it was he who should take them. Neither of them would yield and their mother said: 'My sons, you have divided the pair that contained the jewels and the gold, but no price can be put on this pair and if you cut them in two, the talisman will no longer work. So leave them with me and I'll fetch you food whenever you want and content myself with a mouthful. If you give me any clothes, this will be an act of generosity on your part, and each of you will be able to set up a business in the city. You are my sons and I am your mother, so let us stay as we are for fear of disgrace if your brother happens to return.' They refused to accept this and spent the night quarrelling. One of the king's guards happened to be a guest in a neighbouring house, and when he leaned out of an open window there he heard the whole quarrel and what the two were saying about dividing what they had taken. The next morning this man went to Shams al-Daula, who was king of Egypt at the time, and told him what he had heard. The king sent for the brothers and when they had been brought to him, he had them tortured until they confessed, after which he confiscated the saddlebags and imprisoned them, while making their mother a daily allowance that was sufficient for her needs.

So much for them, but as for Judar, he spent a whole year's service at Suez. Then, when he was at sea, a wind got up which dashed the ship on which he and his companions were sailing against a mountain. The ship broke up, throwing the whole crew into the water, and Judar was the only one to reach land, while all the others died. After he had got ashore, he walked on until he came to a Bedouin camp, and when they asked him about himself, he said that he had been one of the crew of a ship and then told them his story. In their camp was a merchant from Jedda who took pity on him and said: 'Would you like to enter my service, Egyptian, and I'll supply you with clothes and take you with me to Jedda?' Judar agreed to this and went there with the merchant. He was very well treated, and when the merchant then decided to make the pilgrimage he took him with him to Mecca. Once they were there, Judar went off to the sanctuary in order to circumambulate the Ka'ba, and there he came across his friend 'Abd al-Samad, the Maghribi, who was doing the same thing. On seeing Judar, 'Abd al-Samad greeted him and asked him how he was, at which Judar burst into tears and told him what had happened. 'Abd al-Samad took him back to his house, where he gave him a robe of unparalleled splendour and told him: 'Your evil times are over.' He then read Judar's fortune in the sand and told him what had happened to his brothers and how they were imprisoned by the king of Egypt, adding: 'You will be welcome to stay with me until you have finished the pilgrimage ceremonies, and you will meet nothing but good.' 'Sir,' said Judar, 'let me go back to the merchant with whom I came in order to take my leave of him before coming back to you.' 'Do you owe him money?' asked 'Abd al-Samad, and when Judar said no, he told him to go and do this and then come back straight away, adding: 'Decent people recognize their obligation to those who have given them bread.'

So Judar went and took his leave, telling the merchant that he had met his brother. 'Go and fetch him,' said the man, 'and I shall treat him as a guest.' 'There is no need for that,' Judar replied, 'as he is a man of wealth with many servants.' So the merchant gave him twenty dinars, saying: 'This settles my obligations,' and then said good-bye to him. After leaving him, Judar came across a poor man, to whom he gave the dinars, before going on to 'Abd al-Samad, with whom he stayed until the ceremonies were over. 'Abd al-Samad then gave him the ring that he had removed from the treasure of al-Shamardal, telling him to take it, as it would bring him what he wanted. 'It has a servant named al-Ra'd al-Qasif,' he explained, 'and if you need anything in the world and rub the ring, al-Ra'd will appear to you and do whatever you tell him.' He himself then rubbed the ring in front of Judar and al-Ra'd appeared, saying: 'Here I am, master. I shall give you whatever you want. Would you like me to restore a ruined city, ruin one that is flourishing, kill a king or rout an army?' 'Abd al-Samad said: 'Ra'd, this man is now your master, so look after his interests.' He then dismissed him and told Judar: 'When you rub the ring, he will come to you and you can order him to do what you want, as he will never disobey you. So go back to your own country and look after the ring, for you can use it to outwit your enemies, and you should never forget how powerful it is.' 'Sir,' said Judar, 'with your permission I shall go home.' 'Rub the ring, then,' said 'Abd al-Samad, 'and when Ra'd appears, mount on his back, and if you say: "Take me to my own land this very day," that is exactly what he will do.'

After saying goodbye to 'Abd al-Samad, Judar rubbed the ring. Ra'd appeared and said: 'Here I am, master, and I shall give you whatever you want.' 'Take me to Cairo today,' Judar told him. 'That shall be done,' said Ra'd, and he flew off carrying Judar from noon until midnight before setting him down in the courtyard of his mother's house and then leaving. Judar went in to see his mother and when she saw him, she got up and greeted him tearfully, telling him what the king had done to his brothers and how he had had them beaten and had taken the talismanic saddlebags, as well as the bags with gold and jewels. On hearing this, Judar was concerned by his brothers' misfortune, and he told his mother: 'Don't grieve for what has passed, for I shall show you this minute what I can do and I shall fetch my brothers.' He then rubbed the ring and when Ra'd appeared, saying: 'Here I am, master, and I shall give you whatever you want,' Judar said: 'My orders are that you should bring me my two brothers from the king's prison.' Ra'd disappeared into the earth and appeared in the middle of the prison. Both brothers were in great distress and wretchedness because of their sufferings there. They had reached the stage of wishing for death, and one was saying to the other: 'By God, brother, this hardship has lasted too long. How much longer are we going to be imprisoned? Death would come as a relief.' At that moment, the earth opened up and Ra'd came out. He picked them up and descended again into the earth, as they fainted in terror. Then, when they had recovered their senses, they found themselves in their own house with their brother Judar sitting there with their mother beside him. Judar gave them a friendly greeting, but they hung down their heads and began to weep. 'Don't shed tears,' he told them, 'for it was greed and the devil that prompted you to do it. How it was that you came to sell me I do not know, but I console myself with the thought of Joseph, whose brothers, by throwing him into the pit, did more to him than you did to me. Turn to God in repentance and, if you ask His forgiveness, He will forgive you, for He is forgiving and merciful. As for me, I have forgiven you; I welcome you and no harm shall come to you.'

So Judar began to put them at their ease, until they regained their spirits, and he then told them of everything that he had had to endure in Suez until he met the *shaikh* 'Abd al-Samad and of how he had got the ring. 'Don't blame us on this occasion, brother,' they said, 'but if we do the same kind of thing again, then do what you want with us.' 'No harm shall come to you,' Judar repeated, 'but tell me what the king did with you.' 'He had us beaten, threatened us and took the saddlebags,' they told him. 'He will have cause to regret that,' said Judar, who then rubbed the ring. Ra'd appeared, to the consternation of the brothers, who thought that Judar would tell him to kill them. They went to their mother and began to say: 'Mother, we are under your protection; mother, intercede for us.' She told them not to be afraid, and meanwhile Judar told Ra'd to fetch all the jewels that were in the king's treasury, together with whatever else was there, leaving behind nothing at all. He was also to bring the talismanic bags and the pair of bags filled with jewels which the king had taken from his brothers. 'To hear is to obey,' said Ra'd, and he left immediately, collected everything that was in the treasury, as well as the saddle-bags together with their contents, and placed all this in front of Judar. 'Master,' he told him, 'I left nothing behind there.'

Judar told his mother to keep the bag of jewels, but left the talismanic bag in front of him. He then ordered Ra'd to build a high palace that night, gilding it by way of adornment, and supplying it with magnificent furnishings. 'Don't let the sun rise before you have completed it,' he added, and Ra'd promised to have it done. He then disappeared into the earth, after which Judar produced food and they all ate contentedly before falling asleep. As for Ra'd, he collected his *jinn* and told them to build the palace. Some of them cut stones, others did the building, others whitewashed it, others painted it and another group provided the furnishings. By the time day broke, it was ready to the last detail and Ra'd went to Judar and said: 'Master, the palace is finished and complete. Would you like to come and look at it?' Judar, his mother and his brothers all went to look and what they saw was a palace of unmatched splendour, the beauty of whose construction caused the mind to boggle. Judar, who had spent no money on it, was delighted with it, even while he was still outside on the road. He asked his mother whether she was prepared to live in it and she said yes, calling down blessings on him. He then rubbed the ring and Ra'd appeared, saying: 'Here I am.' 'I command you to fetch me forty beautiful white slave girls and forty black ones, together with forty mamluks and forty black slaves.' 'You shall have them,' said Ra'd, and he then went with forty *jinn* to the lands of India, Sind and Persia, carrying off beautiful girls and youths whenever they saw them. He sent another forty, who fetched pretty black girls, and forty who brought black slaves, all of whom were then taken to fill up Judar's palace. He showed them to Judar, who admired them and who told him to fetch robes of the greatest splendour for everyone. 'At your service,' said Ra'd, and Judar went on: 'Bring a robe for my mother to wear and another for me.' Ra'd brought all the robes and Judar distributed them to the slave girls and told them: 'This is your mistress; kiss her hand and do not disobey her, for all of you, white and black alike, are to serve her.' He then gave robes to the mamluks, who kissed his hand, as well as to his brothers. He himself was now like a king with his brothers like viziers, and as his own house was large enough he lodged one of his brothers, with his slave girls, in one part of it, and the other, with his, in another, while he and his mother lived in the new palace, each of them living in his own quarters like a sultan.

As for the king's treasurer, he wanted to take some things out from the treasury, but when he went there he found that it was empty, as in the poet's line:

The hives were full of honey, but when the bees left,
    they were empty.

He gave a loud cry and fell unconscious, and then, when he had recovered his senses, he went out, leaving the door open, and came to King Shams al-Daula to tell him that the treasury had been emptied that night. 'What have you done with the wealth that I had there?' the king demanded. 'By God,' the treasurer told him, 'I didn't do anything to it at all and I don't know how the treasury became empty. Yesterday, when I went in, it was full, but today there was nothing there, although the doors were locked. No one had bored through the wall or broken the lock, so no thief could have got in.' 'Have the saddlebags gone?' the king asked, and when the treasurer said that they had, he nearly went out of his mind. Rising to his feet, he ordered the treasurer to lead the way and then followed him to the treasury, where he found nothing. 'Who has plundered this, showing no fear of my power?' he asked, and overcome with rage and fury he summoned his court. The army leaders came, each thinking that the king was angry with him, but he told them: 'Know that last night my treasury was plundered and I have no idea who could have so little fear of me that he broke in and did this.' 'How could that be?' they asked. 'Ask the treasurer,' the king said, and when they did he told them: 'It was full yesterday, but when I went in today I found it empty, although there was no hole in the wall and the door had not been forced.' They were all astonished to hear that, and none of them had anything to say except for the guard who had earlier informed on Judar's brothers. He went to the king and said: 'King of the age, all last night I watched builders at work and at daybreak I saw a palace of matchless splendour. When I asked about this, I was told that Judar had come back and that it was he who had had the palace built, having brought in mamluks and slaves, as well as providing great sums of money. He freed his brothers from prison and is there in his palace like a sultan.' 'Look in the prison,' ordered the king, but when his men had done this, they brought back word that they had found no trace of the brothers. 'It is clear who is guilty,' the king said, 'for whoever freed them is the man who took my money.' The vizier asked who that was, and the king told him: 'It was Judar, their brother, and he must have taken the saddlebags. So send an emir with fifty men to arrest him and his two brothers; they are to set a seal on all his possessions and to fetch me the brothers to be hanged. Hurry,' he added, for he was still furious, 'send out an emir to bring them to me so that I may have them killed.' 'Be patient,' said the vizier, 'for God is patient and is not quick to punish His servants when they disobey Him. Someone who can have a palace built in a single night, as these people report, can have no match in this world and I'm afraid that the emir may find himself in difficulties because of him. So wait until I can make a plan and we can discover what really happened, so as to ensure that you get what you want, king of the age.' The king agreed to this, and the vizier went on: 'Send the emir to him and invite him here. I shall look after him for you and pretend to be fond of him, asking him about himself. We can then see whether he is strong-willed, in which case we can think of some scheme against him, but if he seems weak-willed, then arrest him and do what you want with him.' 'Send him an invitation,' said the king.

The vizier instructed an emir named 'Uthman to go and invite Judar on behalf of the king to come as his guest, and the king added that 'Uthman was not to fail in this mission. 'Uthman was both stupid and conceited, and when he arrived at Judar's palace he saw a eunuch seated on a chair in front of the door. This man did not get up on his arrival, and in spite of the fact that there were fifty men with 'Uthman, it was as though no one had come. 'Uthman went up to him and said: 'Slave, where is your master?' 'In the house,' the eunuch replied, and as he spoke he continued to lounge on his chair. 'Uthman became angry and said: 'You ill-omened slave, aren't you ashamed to lie there like a good-for-nothing while I'm speaking to you?' 'Be off,' replied the eunuch, 'and don't talk so much.' On hearing this, 'Uthman drew his mace in a rage and was about to strike the 'eunuch', not knowing

that, in fact, he was a devil. When this devil saw him draw
out his mace, he got up, rushed at him, seized it from him
and gave him four blows. His fifty-man escort took this
amiss and drew their swords with the intention of killing
him. 'Are you drawing your swords, dogs?' the latter cried,
and he attacked them, and whoever struck him found
himself crushed with blows from the mace and spattered
with blood. They were all put to flight and they kept on
running as he struck them, until they had fled far away
from the door of the palace, after which their attacker
went back and sat down on his chair, paying no attention
to anyone.

'Uthman and his escort returned, routed and beaten,
and stood in front of the king, to whom they explained
what had happened to them. 'King of the age,' 'Uthman
said, 'when I got to the door of the palace, I saw a eunuch
sitting proudly there on a golden chair. He had been sitting
up, but when he saw me he lay back contemptuously and
did not rise, and when I began to speak to him, he
answered me while still sprawling there. I grew angry and
drew out my mace with the intention of striking him, but
he took it from me and used it to knock me down, after
which he struck my escort and threw them to the ground.
We were powerless against him and so we fled.' The king
was angry and ordered a hundred men to go to the
'eunuch', but when they did and advanced on him, he got
up with his mace and went on striking them until they
ran away from him, after which he went back and sat
down again on his chair. The hundred men returned to
the king and told him what had happened, explaining that
they had run off in fear. The king then sent two hundred,
who suffered the same fate, and after that he said to the
vizier: 'Vizier, I order you to take five hundred men and

bring me this eunuch quickly, together with his master, Judar, and Judar's two brothers.' 'King of the age,' replied the vizier, 'I need no soldiers; I shall go to him alone and unarmed.' 'Go then,' the king told him, 'and do whatever you think appropriate.'

The vizier threw aside his weapons, put on a white robe and took a string of prayer beads in his hand. He walked alone and unaccompanied until he reached Judar's palace, where he saw the 'eunuch' sitting. Unarmed as he was, he then went up to him and sat down beside him with all courtesy, saying: 'Peace be upon you.' 'And upon you, human,' replied the other, adding: 'What is it that you want?' When the vizier heard him say 'human', he realized that this must be a *jinni* and he said, quaking with fear: 'Is your master, Judar, here?' 'Yes,' said the other, 'he is in the palace.' 'Go to him, sir,' said the vizier, 'and tell him that the king Shams al-Daula invites him as a guest, sending him greetings and asking him to honour his house and eat his food.' The doorman said: 'Stay here until I ask him.' The vizier stood there politely as the doorman went into the palace and said to Judar: 'Master, the king sent an emir to you with fifty men, but I beat him and routed them. Then he sent a hundred men, whom I struck, and they were followed by two hundred, whom I drove off. Now it is his unarmed vizier who has come to invite you to a reception. So what do you say?' 'Go and bring the vizier here,' Judar told him, and so the doorman went down and told the vizier to come and speak to his master. 'Willingly,' said the vizier, who then went up to the palace and came into Judar's presence, to find him seated in greater state than the king on a carpet more splendid than any that the king himself could produce. He was bewildered by the beauty of the palace, its decorations

and its furnishings, in comparison with which he himself
looked like a pauper. When he had kissed the ground
before Judar and called down blessings on him, Judar
asked him what his mission was. 'Sir,' replied the vizier,
'your friend the king Shams al-Daula greets you and longs
to see you. He has prepared a reception for you, so will
you set his mind at rest by accepting his invitation?' 'As
he is my friend,' replied Judar, 'take him greetings from
me and ask him to come to me.' When the vizier had
agreed to this, Judar brought out the ring, rubbed it and
told Ra'd, when he appeared, to fetch one of the most
splendid robes. When this had been brought, he told the
vizier to put it on, which he did, and Judar then told him
to go and take his message to the king.

The vizier went off, wearing a more splendid robe than
any he had ever worn before, and when he came into the
presence of the king, he told him about Judar, extolling
the splendour of the castle and its contents. When the
vizier gave him Judar's invitation, the king alerted his
guards, all of whom rose to their feet, and he then ordered
them to mount and to bring him his horse, so that they
might go to Judar. When he himself had mounted, they
all set off for Judar's palace.

Judar himself had told Ra'd: 'I want you to fetch *'ifrits*
in the shape of men from among your *jinn* to stand as
guards in the courtyard of the palace so that the king may
see them. They are to fill him with fear and alarm so as
to make him tremble and realize that my power is greater
than his.' Ra'd produced two hundred *jinn* dressed as
guards, splendidly equipped, powerful and burly. When
the king saw them he was afraid of them, and then, when
he came into Judar's presence, he saw him seated in more
splendour than any king or sultan. He greeted and saluted

him, but Judar did not rise or show him any respect or tell him to be seated, but left him standing.

The king became afraid and could neither sit down nor leave. He started to tell himself: 'If this man were afraid of me, he would not ignore me, and it may be that he is going to punish me because of what I did to his brothers.' At this point, Judar said: 'King of the age, it does not befit someone like you to treat people unjustly and to seize their wealth.' 'Sir,' the king replied, 'do not blame me, for it was greed that forced me to do that, as fate had decreed, but were it not for misdeeds there would be no forgiveness.' He started to apologize for what he had done and to ask for pardon and indulgence, quoting these lines in his appeal:

> Generous son of a noble race, do not blame me for
>   what I did.
> If you wrong me, I forgive you, and if I am in the
>   wrong, please forgive me.

He went on abasing himself before Judar until Judar said: 'May God forgive you,' and told him to sit, which he did. He then produced for him robes as a token of forgiveness, and ordered his brothers to bring out food. After they had eaten, he gave robes to all the king's entourage and treated them honourably, before telling the king to go. He left, but every day he would come back to Judar's palace and it was only there that he would hold his court, as their familiarity and friendship increased.

When this had been going on for some time, the king told his vizier in private that he was afraid that Judar might kill him and seize his kingdom. 'King of the age,' the vizier replied, 'you need have no fear about the kingdom, for what he already has is greater than it and to take it would lessen his authority. If you are afraid that he might kill you, you have a daughter whom you can marry to him so that the two of you will be as one.' The king then asked him to act as a go-between, and the vizier said: 'Invite him here and then we shall spend the evening in one of the rooms. Tell your daughter to put on all her finery and to walk past its door, as when he sees her he will fall in love with her. When we know that he has, I shall go up to him and tell him that she is your daughter, after which I shall lead the conversation on until, before you know anything about it, he will ask you for her hand. When you have given her in marriage to him, you and he will be at one; you will be safe from him and if he should die, you will get a great inheritance from him.' 'That is true, vizier,' said the king, and he arranged for a reception to which he invited Judar.

Judar came to the palace and they all sat until evening in a room there, becoming increasingly friendly with one another. The king had sent to tell his wife to deck the princess out in all her finery and to walk with her past the door of the room. She did what he had told her, and as she went past with her daughter, a girl of matchless beauty and grace, Judar caught sight of her. 'Ah!' he exclaimed as he gazed at her; he became unstrung, being overcome by passionate love and, seized by a rapturous ardour, he turned pale. The vizier said: 'I hope there is nothing wrong, master, but why is it that you seem to have changed and to be in pain?' 'Vizier,' answered Judar, 'whose daughter was that, for she has robbed me of my wits?' 'She is the daughter of your friend the king,' the vizier told him, 'and if you admire her, I shall speak to him and get him to give her to you in marriage.' 'If you do that, I swear by my life that I shall reward you with whatever you want,' promised Judar, adding: 'I shall pay the king whatever he wants by way of a bride price, and we shall be friends and relatives.' 'You are certain to get your wish,' the vizier told him, after which he said in private to the king: 'Judar, your friend, wants a closer link with you, and he has asked me to approach you on his behalf to request the hand of your daughter, the Lady Asiya. Do not disappoint my hopes, but accept my inter-cession and he will pay whatever bride price you want.' 'As for the bride price,' the king replied, 'it has already been paid to me and the girl is one of his servants. I shall give her to him in marriage and he will do me a favour if he accepts.'

The next morning the king summoned a meeting of his court, which was attended by both high and low. The *shaikh* al-Islam was there, and Judar asked for the hand of the princess. The king repeated that the bride price had already been paid, but when the marriage contract had been drawn up, Judar sent for the saddlebag that contained the jewels, which he then presented to the king in return for this. Drums were beaten, pipes sounded and wedding garlands set out, after which Judar slept with his bride. He and the king were then on an equal footing, but after the two of them had stayed together for some time, the king died. The army wanted Judar to take power and, after he had resisted much pressure, he eventually agreed and was installed as ruler. He gave orders for a mosque to be built over the king's tomb, and provided it with endowments.

He ruled for some time with his two brothers as viziers, Salim being vizier of the right and Saliim vizier of the left, but after no more than a year one of them said to the other: 'How long is this going to go on? Are we going to spend all our lives as Judar's servants, without being able to enjoy power or fortune while he is alive? The question is, how can we kill him and take his ring and the saddle-bags?' 'You are more knowledgeable than I am,' said Saliim, 'so think of some way of disposing of him.' 'If I do that,' Salim replied, 'do you agree that I should be the sultan and you the vizier of the right, with the ring and the saddlebags being mine?' 'I do,' his brother answered, and so they agreed to murder Judar because of their love of worldly power. To carry out their plot they told Judar that they wanted to be able to boast that he had come to their house and had been kind enough to accept their hospitality.

They kept on treacherously pressing him to do this until he agreed, and when he asked to whose house he should go, Salim said: 'To mine, and after I have enter-tained you, it will be Saliim's turn.' Judar raised no objec-tion and went with Saliim to Salim's house, where he was offered food in which poison had been put. When he ate it, his flesh decomposed, and Salim got up to remove the ring from his finger. It would not come off and so Salim took his knife and cut away the finger. Then he rubbed the ring and Ra'd appeared, saying: 'Here I am. Ask what you want.' 'Seize my brother and kill him,' Salim told him, 'and then take the two corpses, the one poisoned and the other slain, and throw them down in front of my soldiers.' So Ra'd seized and killed Saliim and then removed the corpses and threw them in front of the army officers, who were sitting eating at a table in the palace. When they saw that Judar and Saliim were dead, they were afraid and stopped eating and asked Ra'd who was responsible for this. 'It was Salim,' Ra'd told them and at that moment Salim came in and said: 'Eat and enjoy yourselves. I have taken the ring from my brother Judar, and this *marid* who is standing before you is the servant of the ring. I ordered him to kill Saliim lest he should attempt to take the kingdom from me as he was a treacherous man and I was afraid that he might play me false. Now that Judar is dead, I am your sultan. Are you going to accept me or shall I rub the ring and have Ra'd kill you, great and small alike?'

'We shall take you as our ruler,' they said. He then ordered that his brothers be buried, and after he had summoned a meeting of his court, some people accompanied the biers and others went in procession ahead. When they returned to the court, Salim took his seat on the throne and they swore allegiance to him. He then told them to draw up a marriage contract between him and Judar's widow. They pointed out that she would have to wait for the legally prescribed period, but he said: 'I know nothing about this period or anything else, and I swear by my life that I shall lie with her tonight.' So they drew up the marriage document and sent to inform the widow of this. 'Invite him to come in,' she said, and when he did, she pretended to be glad and welcomed him warmly, but put poison in the water and so killed him. She took the ring and broke it so that no one should ever own it again and she cut up the saddlebags. Then she sent word to the *shaikh* al-Islam and told the people to make their choice of a king to rule them.

This is the complete story of Judar as it has come down to us.

When she had finished telling this story to King Shahriyar, Shahrazad, seeing it was not yet light, began to recount the story we are now going to hear . . .

Ma'ruf the Cobbler

SHAHRAZAD SAID TO SHAHRIYAR:
A story is also told, O fortunate king, that in Cairo, the guarded city, there was a cobbler named Ma'ruf, who used to patch old shoes. His wife, Fatima, was an evil-minded, vicious and shameless intriguer who was nicknamed 'Dung'. She dominated her husband, and every day she would hurl abuse and a thousand curses at him, while for his part he was afraid of her evil nature and of the harm that she might do him. He was a sensible man, anxious to protect his honour, but he was poor. When he did well in his work, he would spend his earnings on her, but when there was only a little, she would take her revenge on him in the evening, ruining his health and making his night as black as the book of her deeds.* She fitted the poet's lines:

> How many a night have I passed with my wife,
> Spending it in the greatest misery!

* The record kept for each individual and used on the Day of Judgement.

When I first lay with her,
I wish I had brought poison and poisoned her.

One of the things that she did to Ma'ruf was to ask him to bring her a *kunafa* pastry covered with honey in the evening. He said: 'If God helps me to get it, I'll fetch it for you, but today I made no money at all.' 'I don't know what you're talking about,' she said. 'Whether God helps you or not, don't come back to me without it, for if you do, I'll make your night as miserable as your luck was when you married me and fell into my hands.' 'God is generous,' he replied, and he went out, grief oozing from every pore. After he had performed the morning prayer, he opened his shop and prayed: 'My Lord, I implore You to provide me with enough to buy this *kunafa* pastry, so as to save me from the wickedness of that evil woman this evening.' He then sat in his shop until noon without getting any business and becoming more and more afraid of what his wife would do. He got up, locked the shop and began to wonder about the pastry, as he didn't even have enough money to buy bread. He passed by the shop of a *kunafa* seller, and stood there distractedly with his eyes bathed in tears. The shopkeeper noticed him and asked why he was weeping. Ma'ruf told him his story and said: 'My wife is a domineering woman. She has asked me for a *kunafa* pastry, but although I sat in my shop until past noon, I didn't even get the price of a loaf of bread, and I am afraid of her.' The shopkeeper laughed and said: 'No matter! How many *ratls* of pastry do you want?' 'Five,' said Ma'ruf and the man told him: 'I have the butter, but I don't have proper honey but only treacle, although this is better, and what harm would it do if you have the pastry with this?' Ma'ruf was ashamed to object as he was not being pressed to pay, and so he agreed to the treacle. The man cooked him the pastry and drowned it with treacle, making it into a gift fit for a king. 'Would you like some bread and cheese?' he asked, and when Ma'ruf said that he would, he gave him four *nusfs'* worth of bread and half a *nusf'*s worth of cheese, to add to the ten which the *kunafa* cost. 'You owe me fifteen *nusfs,*' he told Ma'ruf, 'but go back to your wife and enjoy yourself. Take this other *nusf* to spend at the baths, and you don't have to repay me for two or three days until God helps you earn some money. There is no need for you to keep your wife short, and I'm prepared to wait until you have some spare cash, over and above what you need for your expenses.'

Ma'ruf took the pastry, the bread and the cheese, and went off contentedly, calling down blessings on his bene-factor and praising God for His goodness. When he got back to his wife, she asked if he had brought the pastry and he said yes, and put it in front of her. When she looked at it and saw that it was coated with treacle, she said: 'Didn't I tell you to bring one made with honey? You haven't done what I wanted – you had it made with treacle.' He tried to excuse himself, pointing out that he had had to buy it on credit. 'Nonsense,' she said. 'I only eat this pastry if it's made with honey.' In her anger she threw it in his face, telling him: 'Go off, you pimp, and get me another!' Then she struck him on the temple and knocked out one of his teeth, so that the blood ran down over his chest. This infuriated him and in return he gave her a light blow on the head, at which she took hold of his beard and started to call for help. The neighbours came in and, after freeing Ma'ruf's beard from her grasp, they began to blame and accuse her, saying: 'All of us are happy to eat this pastry made with treacle. It is disgraceful for

you to bully the poor man like this.' Then they tried to
humour her until eventually they managed to reconcile
husband and wife, but when they had gone she swore that
she wouldn't touch any of the pastry. For his part, Ma'ruf
was suffering from the pangs of hunger and he said to
himself: 'She may have sworn not to eat it, but I shall,'
and he fell to. When she saw him eating, she said: 'God
willing, this food will turn to poison and destroy your
unmentionable body.' 'Not if you say so,' he told her, and
he laughed and went on eating, saying: 'You swore that
you wouldn't eat any of it, but God is generous and if He
wills it, tomorrow night I shall fetch you a honey pastry
and you can eat it all yourself.'

He then tried to console her, but she kept on cursing
him with foul and abusive language all night long. When
morning came, she rolled up her sleeve in order to strike
him, but he said: 'Wait and I'll bring you another pastry.'
He then left for the mosque and, having performed his
prayer, he went on to open his shop, where he took his
seat. He had scarcely settled down before two of the *qadi*'s
officers came to summon him before their master, telling
him that his wife had laid a complaint against him. Recognizing her from the description that they gave, he exclaimed: 'May God bring her misery!' He then got up and
went with the two to the *qadi*, where he found his wife
with her arm bandaged and her veil stained with blood.
She was weeping and wiping away her tears. 'Man,' said
the *qadi*, 'are you not afraid of Almighty God? How can
you strike this woman, breaking her arm, knocking out
her tooth and behaving like this?' 'If I did hit her or knock
out her tooth,' said Ma'ruf, 'then pass whatever sentence
you want on me, but the truth is as follows, and the
neighbours had to make peace between us' – and he told

what had happened from beginning to end. The *qadi* was
a kindly man and he produced a quarter of a dinar and
told Maʿruf to have a honey pastry made for his wife, after
which they could be reconciled. 'Give it to her,' said
Maʿruf, and when she had taken it, the *qadi* tried to
make peace between them. 'Woman,' he said, 'obey your
husband and do you, in turn, be gentle with her.'

After the *qadi* had reconciled them, they left, each going
off in a different direction. Maʿruf went and sat in his shop,
and while he was there the *qadi*'s men came back and
demanded to be paid for their services. 'The *qadi* took
nothing from me,' Maʿruf objected, 'and, in fact, he gave
me a quarter of a dinar.' 'It's no concern of ours whether
he gave or took, but unless you give us our due, we'll take
it from you by force.' They started to drag him around
the market, and in order to give them half a dinar, he had
to sell his tools. When they had left him, he sat sadly,
hand on cheek, for without tools he could do no work.
While he was sitting there, two ugly-looking fellows came
in and told him to report to the *qadi* because his wife had
laid a complaint against him. He told them that the *qadi*
had reconciled them, but they said: 'We are from another
qadi, and she has made her complaint to him.' He went
off with them, calling on God to settle his account with
her, and when he saw her, he said: 'My good woman,
were we not reconciled?' 'There can be no reconciliation
between the two of us,' she replied, at which he went to
the *qadi* and told his story, pointing out that his colleague
had just settled their differences. 'You harlot,' the *qadi*
said, 'in that case, why have you come to complain to
me?' She said: 'He hit me after that,' and the *qadi* said:
'Make it up; don't hit her again and she will not disobey
you again.' When they had been reconciled once more,

the *qadi* told Ma'ruf to pay his officers their fee. He did this and then went back and opened his shop, where he sat like a drunken man, reeling from the worries from which he was suffering.

As he was sitting there, a man came up to him and said: 'Hide yourself, Ma'ruf. Your wife has laid a complaint against you to the High Court and the bailiff is after you.' He got up, locked the shop and fled away in the direction of Bab al-Nasr. All that he had left from the sale of his lasts and his tools were five silver *nusfs*, four of which he used for bread and one for cheese. He was determined to keep out of the way of his wife, but this was on a winter's afternoon and when he came out from among the rubbish heaps, rain poured down on him as though from the mouths of water skins, soaking his clothes. He went to the 'Adiliya mosque and from there he spotted some ruins, among which there was a deserted building that no longer had any door. Wet through as he was, he went in to shelter from the rain, tears pouring from his eyes. He started to complain of his plight, saying: 'Where can I go to escape from that harlot? I pray to God to provide me with someone who might take me to a far-off land where she wouldn't know how to get to me.'

Suddenly, as he was sitting there weeping, the wall split open and out came a tall and ghastly shape. 'Man,' it said, 'why have you disturbed me tonight? I have been living here for two hundred years and I have never seen anyone who came in and acted as you have done. I feel pity for you, so tell me what you want and I shall do it for you.' 'Who and what are you?' Ma'ruf asked him, and he replied: 'I am a *jinni*, the familiar spirit of this place.' Ma'ruf then told him the whole story of his dealings with his wife, and the *jinni* asked: 'Do you want me to take you somewhere

where your wife will not know how to follow you?' 'Yes,' said Maʿruf, at which the *jinni* told him to climb on to his back. When he had done so, the *jinni* carried him off, flying with him from evening until dawn, before setting him down on the summit of a lofty mountain, saying: 'When you go down, you will see the gate of a city. Enter it, and your wife will never know how to find her way to you or be able to reach you.' He then went off, leaving the bewildered Maʿruf there in a state of perplexity until the sun rose. He then told himself: 'I have to get up and climb down to the city, as it won't do me any good to stay sitting here.' When he reached the foot of the mountain, he saw before him a city with high walls, imposing palaces and finely decorated buildings, a delight to the eye. He went in through the city gate, confronting a sight that would gladden the heart of the sorrowful, and as he started to walk through the market, the inhabitants gathered around to look at him, staring in surprise at his clothes, which were not like theirs. One of them asked if he was a stranger, and when he said that he was, the man asked where he had come from. 'From Cairo, the fortunate city,' he said. 'Did you leave it some time ago?' the man said, and when Maʿruf replied: 'Yesterday afternoon,' he laughed and called to the bystanders: 'Come and look at this fellow and hear what he has to say.' 'What does he say?' they asked. 'He claims to be from Cairo and to have left it only yesterday afternoon,' the man told them, at which they all burst out laughing and said: 'Man, are you mad? Do you claim to have left Cairo yesterday afternoon, arriving here this morning, when there is a distance of a full year's journey between the two cities?' 'You are the madmen here, not me,' Maʿruf replied. 'I'm telling the truth; this is Cairene bread which I have with me and it's still fresh.' They started to look at the bread with astonishment, for it was not the same as theirs. The crowd grew bigger and, as people began to tell each other to come and see the bread from Cairo, Ma'ruf became a focus for gossip, with some people believing him and others making fun of him as a liar.

It was at that point that a merchant came up, riding on a mule and followed by two black slaves. He dispersed the bystanders, saying: 'Aren't you ashamed to be crowding around this stranger, making fun of him and laughing at him? What business is it of yours?' He went on heaping blame on them until he had driven them away, as none of them could answer him back. He then said to Ma'ruf: 'Come here, brother. None of this shameless crowd will do you any harm.' He took him off and brought him to a large and ornate house, where he seated him in a parlour fit for a king. On his instructions, his servants opened a chest and brought out a set of clothes such as a rich trader would wear. Ma'ruf was a handsome man, and when he had put these on he looked like a merchant prince. His host called for food and a table laden with all types of splendid dishes was set before them.

When they had eaten and drunk, his host asked his name, to which he replied that he was Ma'ruf, a cobbler by trade, who patched old shoes. 'Where do you come from?' asked his host. 'Cairo,' replied Ma'ruf, to which his host said: 'From what quarter?' 'Do you know Cairo, then?' Ma'ruf asked, to which the man replied that he was himself a Cairene. 'I come from Red Street,' Ma'ruf told him, and when he was asked who he knew there, he gave a long list of names. 'Do you know Shaikh Ahmad, the apothecary?' asked the man. 'He is my next-door neighbour,' Ma'ruf told him. 'Is he well?' was the next question, and when Ma'ruf said that he was, the man went on: 'How many children does he have?' 'Three,' said Ma'ruf. 'Mustafa, Muhammad and 'Ali.' 'And how are they getting on?' the man asked, and Ma'ruf replied: 'Mustafa is doing well as a learned schoolteacher; Muhammad is an apothecary who opened a shop next door to his father after getting married, and his wife has given birth to a son, Hasan.' 'May God bring news as good as this to you yourself,' said the man, and Ma'ruf went on: 'As for 'Ali, he was my boyhood friend. We were always playing together and we used to go to the church disguised as Christians, steal their books and use the money we got from selling them to buy ourselves treats. Once the Christians saw us and caught us with one of their books. They complained to our families, telling 'Ali's father that if he didn't stop his son robbing them, they would lay a complaint before the sultan. To placate them, his father gave him a beating and as a result 'Ali immediately ran away. No one knows where he went and for twenty years he has not been heard of.' 'I am 'Ali, son of Shaikh Ahmad, the apothecary,' said his host, 'and you are my friend Ma'ruf.'

After they had exchanged greetings, 'Ali asked Ma'ruf why he had come there from Cairo, and Ma'ruf told him about his wife, Dung Fatima, and how she had treated him. 'When she had harmed me too many times,' he explained, 'I ran away from her in the direction of Bab al-Nasr. Rain was falling on me and so I went into a deserted building in the 'Adiliya, where I sat weeping. It was then that an *'ifrit*, the familiar spirit of the place, came out and asked me about myself. I told him about the state I was in and he took me on his back and flew with me all night long between the heavens and the earth, before setting me down on the mountain here and telling me about the city. I walked down and when I came into the city, people crowded around me, asking me questions. I told them that I had left Cairo yesterday but they didn't believe me. Then you came and drove them away, after which you brought me here. This is why I left Cairo, but why was it that you came here?' 'Ali said: 'Youthful folly got the better of me at the age of seven, and from then on I wandered from country to country and city to city until I arrived here at Ikhtiyan al-Khutan. I found the people generous and sympathetic, willing to trust a poor man and let him have credit, believing whatever he said. I told them that I was a merchant, that my goods were following on behind me and that I wanted a place where they could be stored. They believed me and cleared out a place for me. I then asked whether anyone would lend me a thousand dinars, to be repaid when my goods came, explaining to them that there were some things that I needed before they arrived. They gave me what I asked for and I set off to the merchants' market, where I found and bought goods. The next day, I sold them at a fifty-dinar profit and bought some more. I began to make friends with the people, winning their affection by generous treatment, and through my trading I made a lot of money. Remember the proverb: "This world is all swagger and deceit." In a place where no one knows you, you can do whatever you want. If you tell everyone who asks that you're a poor cobbler running away from his wife and that you left Cairo yesterday, no one will believe you and you'll be a laughing-stock, however long you stay here. If you say that you were carried by an *'ifrit*, they will shy away; no one will approach you because they'll say that you are possessed and that harm will come to anyone who goes near you. That rumour would be bad for us both, because people know that I myself come from Cairo.'

'What am I going to do, then?' asked Ma'ruf. 'God willing, I'll teach you,' 'Ali replied, and he went on: 'Tomorrow I shall give you a thousand dinars, a mule to ride and a black slave to walk in front of you. He will bring you to the gate of the merchants' market, and when you go in you will find me sitting with them. As soon as I see you, I'll get up to greet you, kissing your hand and making you seem to be a person of the greatest importance. I'll ask you about various types of materials and when I say: "Have you brought such-and-such a fabric with you?" you must tell me that you have a lot of it. If they ask me about you, I shall sing your praises and tell them what a great man you are. I shall say that they should get you a storeroom and a shop, and as I'll stress that you are both rich and generous, whenever a beggar comes up to you, give him what you can. That will lead them to believe me, and as they will be convinced both of your importance and of your generosity, you will win their affection. After that, I shall invite them to a party in your honour and when you meet them, I shall introduce you to them all. You can then start to trade with them and carry on normal business, and in no time you will be rich.'

The next morning, 'Ali handed Ma'ruf the thousand dinars, together with a suit of clothes, mounted him on a mule and gave him a black slave, telling him that there was no need for him to worry about repaying him. 'You are my friend,' he said, 'and it is up to me to treat you generously. Don't trouble yourself; forget how your wife treated you and don't tell anyone about her.' 'May God reward you,' replied Ma'ruf, and mounted the mule. The slave walked in front of him to the merchants' market, where 'Ali was already sitting, surrounded by all the others. Catching sight of the newcomer, he got up and threw himself on him, exclaiming: 'Here is Ma'ruf, the benevolent and generous. What a blessed day this is!' He kissed Ma'ruf's hand in front of all his colleagues, saying: 'Brothers, Ma'ruf the merchant has done you the favour of joining you.'

They greeted him and the respect that 'Ali showed him led them to believe that here was a man of importance. They greeted him after 'Ali had helped him dismount from his mule, and he took them aside privately, one after the other, and started to sing Ma'ruf's praises. 'Is he a merchant?' they asked. 'Yes, indeed,' 'Ali told them. 'He is the greatest of them all, and as far as wealth is concerned, no one has more. His fortune, together with those of his father and his forefathers, is famous among the merchants of Cairo and he has associates in Hind, Sind and Yemen. He is also an extremely generous man and so, bearing in mind the position he holds, you should show him respect and do what you can for him. I can tell you that it is not trade that has brought him here, but an urge to see foreign parts. He doesn't need to leave home to look for profit, as he has so much money that no fire could burn all of it. As for me, I am one of his servants.'

He went on eulogizing Ma'ruf and setting him on a pinnacle above the heads of all others, and his audience started talking to one another about his qualities. They flocked around him, bringing him food and drink for his breakfast, and even the senior merchant came and greeted him. In the presence of the others, 'Ali started to ask: 'Master, have you by any chance brought any material of such-and-such a kind with you?' To which Ma'ruf would answer: 'Yes, I have a lot of it.' Earlier that day 'Ali had showed him various types of costly fabrics and had taught him the names of both what was expensive and what was cheap. So when someone asked whether he had any yellow broadcloth, he said that he had it in quantity, and he gave the same answer when he was asked about cloth that was as red as gazelle's blood, replying in the same way about everything they asked. ''Ali,' said one of the merchants, 'I can see that if this fellow countryman of yours wanted to transport a thousand loads of precious fabrics, he would be able to do it.' 'Ali told him: 'If he took all that from a single one of his warehouses, it would still look full.'

As they were sitting there, a beggar came round the merchants, some of whom gave him various small coins, while most gave nothing at all. When the man came to Ma'ruf, he pulled out a handful of gold coins and passed them over. The beggar called down blessings on him and went off, leaving the admiring merchants to exclaim: 'That was a kingly gift, for he gave the beggar gold without even counting it, something that he would only have done if he were very prosperous and wealthy.' He then gave another handful of gold to a poor woman who approached him, and she too blessed him and went off to tell other poor beggars. These came up one after the other, and 'Ali kept on handing gold to every one of them, until he had given away a thousand dinars.

At that point, he clapped his hands together and recited the formula: 'God suffices for us and to Him we entrust our affairs.' The senior merchant asked him if anything was the matter, to which he replied: 'Most of the people here seem miserably poor and had I known that, I would have brought some money with me in my saddlebags to

give to them. I'm afraid that I may be away from home
for a long time and although it is not in my nature to turn
away a beggar, I haven't any more gold. If one of them
comes up to me, what am I to say to him?' 'Say: "May
God sustain you,"' the man told him, but Ma'ruf objected:
'I am not in the habit of doing that, and this is something
that worries me. What I want is a thousand dinars to give
as alms until my baggage comes.' 'That's no problem,'
the man said, and he sent off one of his servants to fetch
a thousand dinars, which he then presented to Ma'ruf.
Ma'ruf started to give these away to any poor person who
passed by, until the time came for the noon prayer, and
when they all went into the mosque to pray, he scattered
the coins that were left over the heads of the congregation.
When they realized what he was doing, they blessed him,
while the merchants were astonished by his liberality. He
then turned to another one of them, borrowed a thousand
dinars and gave these away as well, while 'Ali looked on,
unable to say a word. This went on until the afternoon
prayer, when Ma'ruf entered the mosque, performed the
prayer and distributed the rest of his money. By the time
that the market was closed, he had received and given
away five thousand dinars. All those from whom he had
borrowed money were told to wait until his goods arrived,
when they could be paid in gold if they wanted or else in
fabrics, if they preferred, from his huge stock.

That evening, 'Ali invited Ma'ruf to a reception with all
the other merchants, seating him in the place of honour.
His talk was all about fabrics and jewels, and whatever
anyone mentioned to him, he claimed to have it in bulk.
The next day, he set out for the market and started turning
to the merchants, borrowing money from them and distributing it to the poor. At the end of twenty days of this he

had borrowed sixty thousand dinars, and no goods had arrived for him nor had anything happened to protect him from his creditors. They, for their part, were getting restive and saying: 'Nothing has come for him,' and asking: 'How long is he going to go on taking people's money and giving it away to the poor?' 'I think that we should talk to 'Ali, his compatriot,' said one of them, and so they went to 'Ali and pointed out that Ma'ruf's goods had not arrived. 'Wait,' 'Ali told them, 'for they are bound to come soon,' but when he was alone with Ma'ruf, he said: 'Did I tell you to toast the bread or to burn it? The merchants are clamouring for their money and they tell me that you owe them sixty thousand dinars, which you have taken and given away to the poor. How can you pay them back, as you are doing no trading?' 'What's all this about?' Ma'ruf asked. 'What is sixty thousand dinars to me? When my goods come, I shall pay them back in fabrics or in gold and silver, whichever they prefer.' 'In God's Name,' 'Ali said, 'do you have any goods?' 'Plenty,' Ma'ruf told him. 'May God and the saints repay you for this disgusting behaviour!' exclaimed 'Ali. 'Wasn't it I who taught you to say this? I'll tell everyone about you.' 'Go away and don't talk so much,' said Ma'ruf. 'Am I a poor man? I have a huge supply of goods and when they come, my creditors will be repaid twice over. I don't need them.' 'Ali grew angry and said: 'You mannerless lout, I'll teach you to tell me shameless lies.' 'Do what you want,' Ma'ruf told him. 'They'll have to wait until my goods arrive, and then they can have what they are owed and more.'

'Ali left him and went off, saying to himself: 'I started by praising him and if I now criticize him, I'll be seen as a liar and fit the proverb: "Whoever follows praise with criticism is a liar twice over."' While he was in this state

of perplexity, the merchants came up and asked if he
had spoken to Ma'ruf. He said: 'I'm too embarrassed to
approach him. He owes me a thousand dinars, but I can't
talk to him about this. You didn't ask my advice when
you gave him money and so you can't blame me for this.
Go and ask him yourselves, and if he doesn't repay you,
then bring a complaint to the king, for if you tell him that
you've fallen victim to a fraudster, he will come to your
rescue.' So they went to the king and explained what had
happened, saying: 'King of the age, we don't know what
to do about this over-generous merchant.' They described
Ma'ruf's behaviour and went on: 'Everything that he gets
he distributes in handfuls to the poor. Were he short of
money, he could never bring himself to give away such
amounts of gold to them, whereas if he is wealthy, then
it is the arrival of his baggage that will show whether he
has been speaking the truth. He claims that he has come
on ahead of it, but we ourselves have seen no trace of it.
Whenever we talk of a certain type of fabric, he claims to
have it in quantity, but although time has passed, we have
heard nothing of the arrival of these goods of his. He owes
us sixty thousand dinars, all of which he has given away
to the poor, who are full of praise for him and extol his
generosity.'

The king was a greedy man, more covetous than
Ash'ab,* and when he heard how generous Ma'ruf was,
his greed was aroused and he said to his vizier: 'If this
merchant were not a very wealthy man, he would not be
so generous. His baggage is bound to come, and when
these merchants gather around him he will distribute large

---

* Ash'ab was a notoriously greedy servant of the caliph 'Uthman
(644–55).

sums of money to them, money to which I have a better right. I want to make a friend of him and take him as a companion until his baggage arrives, and then I shall get whatever he gives them. He can have my daughter as his wife and I shall add his wealth to my own.' 'King of the age,' said the vizier, 'in my opinion this man is a fraudster and fraudsters bring ruin on the houses of the covetous.'

The king said: 'I shall test him, vizier, and find out whether he is a cheat or a truthful man and whether he has been brought up in luxury or not.' When the vizier asked how he proposed to do that, the king said: 'I shall send him a summons and when he comes here and sits down, I shall treat him politely and give him a jewel that I have. If he recognizes what it is and how much it is worth, then he must be a rich and prosperous man, but if he doesn't, then he is a fraud and a parvenu and I shall have him put to the worst of deaths.'

Ma'ruf went to the palace in answer to a summons from the king. They exchanged greetings and the king seated him at his side. 'Are you Ma'ruf the merchant?' he asked, and when Ma'ruf said yes, the king went on: 'The merchants claim that you owe them sixty thousand dinars. Is what they say true?' Ma'ruf confirmed that it was, and when the king asked why he did not repay them, he replied: 'When my baggage train arrives, I'll give them twice as much as I owe, and they can have it in gold, silver or goods, whichever they prefer. Whoever is owed a thousand dinars will get two thousand back, because he saved me from disgracing myself among the poor, for I am a man of substance.' The king then said: 'Take this jewel and tell me what kind it is and what is its worth.' He handed over a gem the size of a hazelnut which he had bought for a thousand dinars; he was very proud of

it, having no other like it. Ma'ruf took it in his hand and
squeezed it between his thumb and forefinger. It proved
too delicate to bear the pressure and so it shattered. 'Why
have you destroyed my jewel?' asked the king, but Ma'ruf
only laughed and said: 'King of the age, that was no jewel,
but only a bit of mineral worth a thousand dinars. How
can you call it a jewel, when a real jewel is something
worth seventy thousand? This can only be described as a
piece of mineral, and I myself am not concerned with any
gem that is not the size of a walnut, since for me such a
thing is valueless. How can you be a king and call a
thousand-dinar piece like this a gem? You have an excuse,
however, as your people are poor and have no valuable
treasures.' The king said: 'Do you have any of the kind of
jewels you have talked about?' and when Ma'ruf claimed
to have many of them, greed got the better of him and he
asked: 'Will you give me some of these real ones?' 'When
my baggage comes, you can have them in plenty,'
promised Ma'ruf, 'and as I have quantities of whatever
you can ask for, I shall not charge you anything for them.'
The delighted king dismissed the other merchants, telling
them to wait until Ma'ruf's baggage arrived, when they
could come back and he personally would pay them off.
They then left.

So much for Ma'ruf and the merchants, but as for the
king, he went to the vizier and told him to talk with
Ma'ruf in a friendly way and to tell him about the king's
daughter, so that a marriage might be arranged that would
allow them to share in his fortune. The vizier said: 'King
of the age, there is something about this man that I don't
like. I think that he is a fraud and a liar, and I advise you
not to talk like this, lest you lose your daughter for no
return.' The vizier himself had earlier asked for the hand

of this princess and her father had been ready to give her to him, but when she heard of it she had refused to accept him. So now the king said: 'Traitor, you don't want any good to come to me because my daughter turned you down when you asked for her hand. You hope to stand in the way of her marriage and would like her to stay unwed in order to give you a chance of winning her yourself. Listen to what I have to say. This is nothing to do with you and how can this man be a cheat and a liar? He could tell the price that I paid for my jewel and he broke it because he didn't like it. He has quantities of jewels and when he marries my daughter and sees how lovely she is, she will charm him, and in his love for her he will shower her with gems and treasures. What you want to do is to deprive both her and me of all these good things.'

The vizier stayed silent, as he was afraid of the king's anger, but he said to himself: 'Set the dogs on the cows.' He then made a friendly approach to Ma'ruf and said: 'His majesty is fond of you and he has a beautiful daughter whom he would like to marry to you. What have you to say?' Ma'ruf agreed to the offer, but added: 'Wait until my baggage arrives, for royal princesses need large dowries suitable for their rank and condition. At the moment I have no money, and the king had better wait until my goods come. As I am a rich man, for the princess's dowry I shall give five thousand purses of gold, and then I shall have to have a thousand purses to distribute to the poor and needy on the wedding night, with a thousand more for those who walk in the wedding procession. With another thousand I shall give a banquet to the troops and others, and I must have a hundred gems to present to the bride on the morning after the wedding, as well as a hundred for the slave girls and the eunuchs, since each of them must have one as a token of the bride's high rank. Then I shall need to clothe a thousand of the naked poor, as well as giving alms. This cannot be done until my baggage comes, but when it does, as I have plenty, I shan't have to worry about these expenses.'

The vizier went off and told all this to the king, who said: 'If this is what he proposes to do, how can you say that he is a fraudster and a liar?' 'I still do,' insisted the vizier, but the king reprimanded him harshly, swearing to kill him if he did not stop. He then told him to go back and bring Ma'ruf to him, saying that he would arrange things himself.

The vizier went to tell Ma'ruf of the king's summons. 'To hear is to obey,' Ma'ruf replied, and when he came, the king told him: 'Don't make this excuse. My own treasury is full, so take the keys: spend all you need; give away what you want; clothe the poor and do as you please. There is no need for you to concern yourself about the princess and the slave girls, for when your baggage comes you can be as generous as you like with your wife, and, until this happens, I am prepared to wait for her dowry, and I shall never be separated from you.' On his instructions, Shaikh al-Islam drew up a marriage contract between his daughter and Ma'ruf and began to prepare the wedding celebrations. The town was adorned with decorations, drums were beaten and tables laid with foods of all kinds. Performers arrived and Ma'ruf sat on a chair in a room with players, dancers, gymnasts, jugglers and mountebanks exhibiting their skills before him. On his instructions, the treasurer would fetch gold and silver and he would go round the audience with handfuls of money for the performers, gifts for the poor and needy and clothes for the naked.

This was a noisy celebration and the treasurer could scarcely keep up with the demands on the treasury's reserves, while as for the vizier, his heart was almost bursting with rage yet he could not speak. 'Ali was astounded at the amount of money being given away and he exclaimed: 'May God and the saints split your head, Ma'ruf! Wasn't it enough for you to waste the money of the merchants, that you had to do the same to the wealth of the king?' 'That is nothing to do with you,' replied Ma'ruf, 'and when my baggage comes, I'll give him back twice as much.' So he went on throwing away the money, telling himself: 'Something will happen to protect me; what will be will be, for no one can escape fate.'

The celebrations carried on for forty days and on the forty-first a magnificent bridal procession was organized, with all the emirs and the soldiers walking in front of the bride. When they brought her to Ma'ruf, he began to scatter gold over the heads of the people and huge amounts of money were spent. He was then escorted to the princess and took his seat on a high couch; the curtains were lowered, the door shut and everyone there went out, leaving Ma'ruf with his bride. For a time he sat there sadly, striking one hand against the other and reciting the formula: 'There is no might and no power except with God, the Exalted, the Omnipotent.' 'God preserve you, my master,' said the princess. 'Why are you so sad?' 'How can I fail to be sad,' he told her, 'when your father has thrown me into confusion? What he has done to me is like burning crops while they are still green.' 'What is it that he has done?' she asked. 'Tell me.' Ma'ruf explained: 'He has brought me to you before my baggage has arrived. I had wanted to have at least a hundred jewels to distribute to your maids, one for each of them, so that they might have the pleasure of saying: "My master gave this to me on the night he went in to my lady." This is something that would have added to your status and increased your reputation. Because I have so many jewels, I have not been accustomed to limiting myself when it comes to giving them away.' The princess replied: 'There is no need to vex yourself or to worry about that. I'm not going to hold it against you and I can wait until your baggage arrives, while as for my maids, you needn't bother about them. Take off your clothes now and relax, for when your goods are here, we can get the jewels and whatever else there is.'

So Ma'ruf got up and undressed before sitting back on the couch in order to dally and play with his bride. He put his hand on her knee and she sat down on his lap, thrusting her lip into his mouth. This was an hour to make a man forget his father and his mother. He put his arms around her, squeezing her tightly and drawing her close to his breast. He sucked her lip until honey dripped from her mouth, and when he put his hand beneath her left armpit, both their bodies felt the urge for union. He touched her between her breasts before moving his hand down between her thighs. He got between her legs and set about the two tasks, exclaiming: 'Father of the two veils!' before priming the charge, lighting the fuse, adjusting the compass and then applying the fire. All four corners of the tower were demolished as the strange adventure, which none can question, took place and as the bride gave the shriek that is unavoidable, Ma'ruf took her virginity. This was a night standing outside the ordinary span of life, comprising, as it did, the union of beauties, with embraces, love-play, sucking and copulation lasting until morning. Ma'ruf then got up and went to the baths, from which he emerged wearing a royal robe. When he entered the audience chamber, all present rose to their feet to greet him respectfully and courteously, congratulating him and calling down blessings on him. He took his seat beside the king and asked: 'Where is the treasurer?' 'Here he is in front of you,' they told him, and he then gave instructions that robes of honour were to be given to all the viziers, emirs and officers of state. When all that he asked for had been fetched, he sat distributing gifts to everyone who came to him, in accordance with the man's status.

Things went on like this for twenty days, during which neither his baggage nor anything else made its appearance. The treasurer became extremely disgruntled and approached the king when Ma'ruf was absent and the king and the vizier were sitting by themselves. He kissed the ground before the king and said: 'King of the age, there is something that I must tell you, as you might blame me if I failed to bring it to your notice. You should know that the treasury is empty, or rather there is so little money left there that in ten days' time there will be none at all and we shall have to close it.' The king turned to the vizier and said: 'My son-in-law's baggage has been delayed and there has been no news of it,' but the vizier laughed and said: 'May God deal kindly with you, king of the age. You don't realize what this lying trickster is doing. I take my oath that he has no baggage at all, and there is no plague to get rid of him for us. He has gone on and on playing his tricks on you until he has managed to squander your riches and marry your daughter, all for nothing. How long will you let him get away with it?' The king asked how he could find out the real truth and the vizier told him: 'The only person who can discover a man's secrets is his wife. Send for your daughter to come and sit behind the curtain here so that I can ask her how things really stand and get her to test him and find out how he is placed.' 'There can be no harm in that,' the king said, adding, 'and I swear that if I discover him to be an impostor, I shall put him to the foulest of deaths.'

He brought the vizier to his sitting room and then sent for his daughter. She came and sat behind the curtain, all this being while Ma'ruf was away. She asked her father what he wanted and he told her to speak to the vizier. When she put the question to him, he said: 'My lady, you must know that your husband has squandered your father's wealth and has married you without paying a dowry. He keeps on making promises to us, but he never keeps them; there is no news of his baggage and, in short, we want you to tell us about him.' 'He talks a lot,' she replied, 'but although he is forever coming to me and promising me jewels, treasures and precious stuffs, I've not seen anything.' The vizier asked: 'My lady, could you discuss things with him this evening in the give-and-take of conversation? Get round to saying: "Don't be afraid to tell me the truth. You are my husband and I would do nothing to hurt you. If you tell me how things really stand, I'll think of some way to get you out of your difficulties." Then say whatever you think best as you talk to him and let him see that you love him. If you get him to confess, come and tell us the truth.' 'I know how to test him, father,' she agreed.

She went off and after supper when her husband came to her, as usual, she got up and, putting her arms under his, she did her best to ensnare him – and how well women are able to do this when there is something they want from a man! She went on flattering him with words that were sweeter than honey until she had stolen away his

wits. When she saw that he was entirely taken up with
her, she said: 'My darling, the delight of my eyes and the
fruit of my heart, may God never deprive me of you and
may Time never separate us. Love for you has lodged in
my heart; the fire of my passion for you has consumed
my entrails and I can never fail in my duty towards you.
I want you to tell me the truth, for lying is unhelpful as it
can never succeed all the time. How long are you going
to go on trying to trick my father? I'm afraid that you
will be exposed before I can think of some plan, and
he will use violence against you. If you tell me the truth,
all will be well for you and you need fear no harm. How
many times are you going to claim to be a wealthy
merchant with a baggage train on the way? You have been
talking again and again about this baggage for a very long
time, but no word has come of it and your face shows
how worried you are. If it's not true, tell me and, God
willing, I shall think of some way to get you out of the
difficulty.' 'My lady,' he replied, 'I shall tell you the truth
and you can then do whatever you want.' 'Tell me, then,'
she said, 'but be sure to stick to the truth, for this is the
vessel of salvation, and beware of lying, which disgraces
the liar. How well the poet has put it:

> Stick to truth even though it threatens you with death
>   by fire;
> Seek God's approval, for the foolish man
> Angers his Lord and seeks to please His slaves.'

Ma'ruf then said: 'I must tell you, my lady, that I am
not a merchant; I have no baggage and there is nothing
to protect me from my creditors. In my own land I was a
cobbler and I had a wife known as Dung Fatima' – and he
went on to tell her the story of his dealings with Fatima

from beginning to end. She laughed and said: 'What a good liar and trickster you are!' 'My lady,' he said, 'God preserve you as a keeper of shameful secrets and a remover of anxieties.' She said: 'You duped my father and deceived him with all your bragging so that, thanks to his greed, he married me off to you and you then squandered his money. The vizier holds this against you and on innumerable occasions he has told my father that you are a fraud and a liar. My father has refused to accept this because the vizier once asked for my hand and I wouldn't take him as a husband. Now, as time goes on, my father finds himself in difficulties, and he has asked me to get you to confess. I've done that and your cover has been removed. That would make my father determined to do you a mischief, but I have become your wife and I'm not going to neglect you. If I tell him, he will know for certain that you are a swindler and a liar who has tricked princesses and wasted the wealth of kings. For him that would be an unforgivable sin and he would be certain to have you put to death. Then everybody would know that I married a fraud and I would be disgraced. Also, if my father has you killed, he may try to marry me to another man and that is something that I shall never accept, even if it costs me my life. So now get up, dress yourself as a mamluk, take fifty thousand dinars of my money and ride off on a good horse to some place where my father's writ does not run. You can set up as a merchant there and you must then write me a letter, giving it to a courier who is to deliver it to me secretly, so that I may know where you are. Then I'll send you whatever I can lay my hands on and you will be a wealthy man. When my father dies, I'll send for you and you can return with all honour and respect, while if either you or I die and are gathered into God's mercy, we shall be reunited on the Day of Resurrection. This is the right course to follow and as long as we both remain well, I shall not stop sending you letters and money. Now get up before day breaks and you find yourself at a loss, with destruction facing you on every side.' He said: 'My lady, I am under your protection. Let me lie with you before we say goodbye.' 'There's no harm in that,' she replied and so he lay with her, and then washed, before dressing as a mamluk. He told the grooms to saddle him a good horse and, having taken leave of his wife, he left the city as night was ending and rode away. Everyone who saw him thought that he must be one of the king's mamluks going out on an errand.

In the morning, the king, with his vizier, came to the sitting room and sent for the princess, who arrived behind the curtain. 'What have you to say?' her father asked her and she replied: 'I say: "May God blacken the face of the vizier in the same way that he would have disgraced me in the eyes of my husband."' When her father asked about this, she said: 'He came to me yesterday, but before I could say anything to him about this, in came Faraj the eunuch with a letter in his hand. He said: "There are ten mamluks standing beneath the palace window. They gave me this letter and told me: 'Kiss the hands of our master, Ma'ruf the merchant, for us and give him this letter. We are some of the mamluks who were with his baggage train, and when we heard that he had married the king's daughter, we came to tell him what happened to us on the way.'" I took the letter and when I read it I found that it ran: "From the five hundred mamluks to our master, Ma'ruf the merchant. To continue: we have to tell you that after you left us, we were attacked by mounted Bedouin. There were some two thousand of them against our five hundred. There was a fierce battle, as they blocked our way and we had to go on fighting them for thirty days. This is why we have been so slow in reaching you. The Bedouin took two hundred loads of fabrics from the baggage and killed fifty of us." When my husband heard the news, he cursed the mamluks and exclaimed: "How could they fight with Bedouin for the sake of a mere two hundred loads of goods? How much is that? They shouldn't have wasted time on that, as the two hundred loads would be worth no more than seven thousand dinars. I shall have to go to them and hurry them on. What was taken will not diminish the baggage train or have any effect on me, and I can count it as alms given by me to the Bedouin." He was laughing as he left me and showing no signs of distress either at the goods that he had lost or at the death of his mamluks. When he went down, I looked out of the palace window and saw the ten mamluks that had brought the letter. They were splendid as moons, and my father has none like them; while the robes that they were wearing were each worth two thousand dinars. My husband went off with them in order to fetch his goods, and thank God I never had the chance to say anything about what you told me to ask him, as he would have laughed at me and at you and he might have begun to disparage me and to hate me. All the fault lies with your vizier who keeps on speaking improperly about my husband.' The king said: 'Daughter, your husband is a very wealthy man who never thinks about money. From the first day that he came here, he has been giving it away to the poor and, God willing, his baggage will arrive soon to our great benefit.' He was completely taken in by her scheme and kept on trying to reassure her, while heaping abuse on the vizier.

So much for the king, but as for Ma'ruf, he rode off through the desert in a state of confusion, not knowing where to go. He was distressed by the pain of parting from his wife and, faced with the torments of passion, he recited:

Time has betrayed our union and separated us;
The harshness of parting burns my heart until it
    melts.
My eyes shed tears at the loss of the beloved:
Now we are parted; when shall we meet again?
You moon that gleams so brightly, I am he
Whose heart is torn in pieces by your love.
I wish I had not met you even once,
For, after union, I have tasted pain.
My love for Dunya stays with me always,
And if I die of love, may she survive.
O brilliance of the radiant sun, shine on
A heart love's former favours have consumed.
Will days to come unite us once again,
Allowing us to meet in joyfulness,
Happy within her palace, where I may
Clasp in my arms the sand hill's branch?
You are the moon, whose sun sheds light,
And may your lovely face not cease to shine.
I am content with the distress of love,
For love's good fortune is pure misery.

When he had finished these lines, he shed bitter tears and, as he could see nowhere to go, he decided that death was preferable to life. In his perplexity, he wandered on like a drunkard and did not stop until noon, when he had come to a small village. Near it he could see a peasant ploughing with two oxen, and as he was very hungry, he

went up to him. After the two of them had exchanged
greetings, the peasant said: 'Welcome, master. Are you
one of the king's mamluks?' Ma'ruf said that he was
and he was then invited to eat at the peasant's house.
Recognizing that here was a generous man, he said:
'Brother, I don't see that you have anything to give me to
eat, so how can you invite me?' 'There are good things
here, master,' the peasant told him, 'for the village is close
at hand. Do you dismount and I'll go and fetch food for
you and fodder for your horse.' 'If it's as near as that, I
can get there as fast as you,' said Ma'ruf, 'and I can then
buy what I want from the market and eat it.' The peasant
said: 'It's only a little place with no market, and nobody
trades there, so I beg you to do me the favour of staying
with me. I'll go there and be back soon.'

Ma'ruf dismounted and the peasant started off to the
village to fetch food, leaving him sitting there to wait for
him. Ma'ruf said to himself: 'I've turned this poor fellow
away from his work and so I'd better get up and do his
ploughing for him, to let him have something in return
for the time that I've made him waste.' He took hold of
the plough and drove the oxen forward, but before he had
gone far, the plough snagged on an obstacle. The oxen
stopped, and for all his efforts Ma'ruf couldn't get them
to move on. He looked at the plough and found that it
had caught on a golden ring. Then, when he cleared the
earth from round it, he found that the ring was set in the
middle of a marble slab as big as a millwheel. He worked
at it until he succeeded in shifting it and under it he
discovered steps leading down into an underground
chamber. Down he went and there he found a place as
big as a bath house, with four side chambers. Of these,
the first was filled from top to bottom with gold; the

second held emeralds, pearls and corals; the third was full of sapphires, hyacinth gems and turquoises; while in the fourth were diamonds and various other types of precious stones. At the head of the room was a chest made of clear crystal, filled with unique gems, each as big as a walnut, and sitting on top of this was a small golden casket, the size of a lemon.

Maʿruf was astonished and delighted by what he saw, but he wondered what could be in the casket. He opened it and discovered a golden ring inscribed with names and talismans in a script that looked like ants' tracks. He rubbed the ring and immediately a voice was heard saying: 'Here I am, master. Whatever you ask will be given you. Do you want to build a town, destroy a city, have a canal dug or anything else of the kind? Whatever you ask will be done, through the permission of the Omnipotent God, the Creator of night and day.' 'Who and what are you, creature of my Lord?' asked Maʿruf, and the voice replied: 'I am the servant of the ring, bound to the service of its owner. I shall perform whatever task you ask of me, and I can have no excuse for not doing so as I am lord of the races of the *jinn*, with seventy-two tribes under my command, each numbering seventy-two thousand. Each of these controls a thousand *marids*; each *marid* controls a thousand *ʿauns*; each *ʿaun* controls a thousand devils and each devil controls a thousand *jinn*. All of these owe me allegiance and none of them can disobey me. I am bound to this ring by a spell and I cannot disobey its owner. You are now the owner and I am your servant, so ask whatever you want and I shall hear and obey you. Whenever you need me, whether on land or in the sea, rub the ring and you will find me with you, but take care not to rub it twice in a row or else fire from the names engraved on it will burn me up and you will have cause to regret my loss when I am dead. This is all that I have to tell you about myself.'

'What is your name?' asked Ma'ruf, and the servant of the ring told him that it was Abu'l-Sa'adat. 'What is this place, Abu'l-Sa'adat,' he asked, 'and whose spell imprisoned you in this casket?' Abu'l-Sa'adat replied: 'This is known as the treasure chamber of Shaddad ibn 'Ad, who built Iram, City of the Columns, whose like has never been created in any land.* While Shaddad lived, I was his servant and this was his ring; he put it among his treasures but it has now fallen to your lot.' Ma'ruf asked him: 'Can you bring all this treasure to the surface?' 'With the greatest of ease,' replied Abu'l-Sa'adat, at which Ma'ruf instructed him to bring out the whole of it, leaving nothing behind. Abu'l-Sa'adat pointed at the ground, which split open and into which he disappeared briefly, before two graceful and handsome young boys emerged, carrying golden baskets, themselves filled with gold. They emptied out the baskets, went off and fetched more, and kept on bringing up gold and jewels until, before an hour was up, they announced that there was nothing left in the treasure chamber. Abu'l-Sa'adat himself then came out and said: 'Master, I have checked and we have removed everything that was there.' 'Who are these handsome boys?' Ma'ruf asked him, to which he replied: 'They are my sons. I didn't think it worthwhile summoning the *'auns* for a task like this, so my sons have done what you wanted and they are honoured to have been of service to you. Now ask for something else.'

Ma'ruf said: 'Are you able to fetch me mules and chests,

* Quran 89.6–7.

and can you then put the money in the chests and load them on the mules?' 'Nothing could be easier,' replied Abu'l-Sa'adat, who then gave a great cry, at which all eight hundred of his sons appeared in front of him. He told them: 'Some of you are to change into mules, while others are to become handsome mamluks, even the least of whom is to be better than any found with kings; some are to be muleteers and others servants.' They did what he told them, with seven hundred becoming mules and the rest servants. Abu'l-Sa'adat then summoned the *'auns* and, when they came, he ordered some of them to turn into horses, with golden saddles encrusted with gems. When Ma'ruf saw this, he asked: 'Where are the chests?' and after these had been fetched, he gave instructions that the gold and the various precious stones were to be packed separately. The chests were then loaded on to three hundred mules.

Then Ma'ruf asked Abu'l-Sa'adat whether he could fetch him bales of costly fabrics, and when he was asked whether he wanted these from Egypt, Syria, Persia, India or Rum, he said: 'Bring me a hundred bales from each of them, carried on a hundred mules.' 'Allow me time to arrange for my *'auns* to do that, master,' Abu'l-Sa'adat replied, and he then instructed each group of *'auns* to go to a different land to get what was needed; they were then to take the shape of mules and come back carrying the goods. 'How long do you need?' Ma'ruf asked, and Abu'l-Sa'adat said: 'However long it remains dark, for by dawn you shall have all that you want.' After Ma'ruf had agreed to this, Abu'l-Sa'adat gave orders that a tent was to be pitched for him and, when this had been done, a table laden with food was brought in. 'Take your seat in this tent, master,' said Abu'l-Sa'adat. 'You need have no fear, as my sons here will guard you, while I go to collect my *'auns* and send them off to carry out your wishes.'

When Abu'l-Sa'adat had left, Ma'ruf sat in the tent with the food in front of him and Abu'l-Sa'adat's sons standing there in the shape of mamluks, servants and retainers. While he was seated in state, up came the peasant carrying a big bowl of lentils and a horse's nosebag full of barley. When he saw the tent with the mamluks standing with their hands on their breasts, he thought that the king must have come and halted there. He stopped, flabbergasted, saying to himself: 'I wish I had killed a couple of chickens and roasted them with cow's butter for the king.' He was intending to go back to do this in order to entertain the king, when Ma'ruf caught sight of him and called out to him. He then told the mamluks to fetch him and they brought him up, together with his bowl of lentils. 'What's this?' Ma'ruf asked him, and he said: 'This is your meal and here is fodder for your horse. Don't blame me, for I never thought that the king would come here. Had I known, I would have killed a couple of chickens and prepared a better meal.' 'The king has not come,' Ma'ruf told him. 'I am his son-in-law, but I quarrelled with him and he sent his mamluks to reconcile me with him. I'm on my way back to the city, but as you have produced this food for me without knowing who I was, I shall accept what you have brought. Even if it is lentils, this and only this is what I intend to eat.' He told the peasant to put the bowl in the middle of the table and ate from it until he had had enough, while the peasant ate his fill from the other splendid dishes that were there. Ma'ruf then washed his hands, and after he had allowed the mamluks to eat, they finished off what was left on the table. Then, when the peasant's bowl had been emptied, Ma'ruf filled it with gold and said: 'Take this home with you and then come to visit me in the city, where I shall treat you generously.' The man took the bowl, brimming with gold, and drove his two oxen back to the village as proudly as if he were cousin to the king.

Ma'ruf passed a night of unalloyed pleasure. The brides of the treasure* were brought for him and beat their tambourines, all the while dancing in front of him, making it a night that stood outside the ordinary span of life. The next morning, before he knew what was happening, a cloud of dust could be seen rising and when it cleared away there were seven hundred mules carrying bales of fabric, surrounded by servants – muleteers, baggage handlers and torch-bearers – with Abu'l-Sa'adat mounted on a mule playing the part of baggage master. In front of him was a palanquin with four ornamented poles of glistening red gold, set with gems. When he reached Ma'ruf's tent, he dismounted, kissed the ground and said: 'All that you asked for has been done. In this palanquin is a set of robes from the treasure chamber, the like of which no king possesses. Put it on; then get into the palanquin and tell us what you want done.'

Ma'ruf said: 'I want to write a letter for you to take to the city of Ikhtiyan al-Khutan, where you must go to my relative, the king, whose presence you are to enter in the shape of a human courier.' 'To hear is to obey,' said Abu'l-Sa'adat, and when Ma'ruf had written his letter and sealed it, he took it away and brought it to the king. He found the king telling the vizier: 'I'm worried about my son-in-law, as I'm afraid that the Bedouin may kill him. I wish that I knew where he has gone so that I could follow

---

* Beautiful guardians of magical treasure troves.

him with my troops, and I wish that he had told me before going.' 'May God be gentle to you in your foolishness,' the vizier replied. 'I swear that the man realized that we had woken up to what he was doing and then ran away, fearing disgrace, for he is nothing but a trickster and a liar.' It was at this point that the 'courier' came in, kissing the ground before the king and praying that he be granted long life as well as continued glory and prosperity. 'Who are you and what do you want?' asked the king, and the 'courier' said: 'I am a messenger sent to you by your son-in-law, who is on his way with his baggage train. He sent me with a letter for you, and here it is.'

The king took the letter and, on reading it, he found the following: 'The best of greetings to my uncle, the great king. I have arrived with my baggage, so come out and meet me with your troops.' 'May God blacken your face, vizier!' exclaimed the king. 'How many times have you cast aspersions on my son-in-law's honour, calling him a fraud and a liar? Here he is with his baggage, while you are nothing but a traitor.' The vizier looked down at the ground in shame and embarrassment and replied: 'King of the age, I only said that because his baggage took so long in coming, and I was afraid that all the money he spent would be lost and gone.' 'Traitor!' said the king. 'What is my wealth in comparison with what he is bringing? He is going to repay me many times over.' He ordered the city to be adorned with decorations and then went to his daughter and said: 'I have good news for you. Your husband is close at hand, bringing his baggage with him. He has sent me a letter to tell me about it, and I'm just on my way off to meet him.' The princess was astonished by this and said to herself: 'How amazing! I wonder if he was making a fool of me and laughing at me, or else testing me by telling me that he was a poor man. God be praised that I didn't fail in my duty to him.'

So much for Maʿruf, but as for ʿAli the merchant, he saw the decorations in the city and asked about them. When people told him: 'The baggage of Maʿruf the merchant, the king's son-in-law, has arrived,' he exclaimed: 'Great God, what calamity is this? He came as a poor man, running away from his wife, so how can he have got hold of baggage? It may be that the princess did something for him so as to avoid disgrace, as there is nothing that kings cannot do. At any rate, may God shelter him and preserve him from shame.'

All the other merchants were pleased and delighted at the prospect of getting their money back, and the king, for his part, collected his troops and went out. Abu'l-Saʿadat had come back to say that he had delivered the letter, and Maʿruf gave the command: 'Load up.' Wearing his treasure-hoard robes he mounted his palanquin and moved off in a thousand times greater and more imposing state than the king. When he had got halfway, the king met him with his men, and on his arrival, when he saw the robes Maʿruf was wearing and the palanquin in which he was riding, he threw himself on him, greeting him and praying that God preserve him. Every notable in the state joined in the greeting, as it was clear that Maʿruf had been telling the truth and that there was nothing false about him.

He entered the city in a procession splendid enough to cause the gall bladder of the envious to burst, and the merchants hurried up to kiss the ground before him. ʿAli the merchant said to him: 'You have made a success of this, master of impostors, but you deserve your success, and may God in His grace grant you even more.' Maʿruf laughed, and when he had entered the palace and taken his seat on the throne, he said: 'Place the gold in the treasury of my uncle, the king, and bring me the fabrics.' These were fetched by the servants, who started to open the bales, one after another, until, when seven hundred had been unpacked, he picked out the best and ordered that they be taken to the princess to distribute among her maids. He also sent her the contents of a chest, full of jewels, which were to be brought to her to be given to the eunuchs as well as the maids. The merchants to whom he owed money were repaid in fabrics and whoever had lent him a thousand dinars was given what was worth two thousand dinars or more. After that, he began to distribute money to the poor and needy, while the king, who was watching, was unable to object. This went on until he had given away everything that had been in the seven hundred bales and it was then that he turned to the soldiers, to whom he gave precious stones – emeralds, sapphires, pearls, corals, and so on. He gave away gems in handfuls, without counting, and the king said: 'That's enough, my son; there is nothing much left of your goods.' 'I have plenty,' said Ma'ruf, and as it was clear that he had been speaking the truth, no one could think that he was now lying and he, for his part, didn't care what he gave away, as Abu'l-Sa'adat could fetch him whatever he wanted.

The treasurer now came to the king and said: 'King of the age, the treasury is full and there is no room for the remaining gold and jewels. Where are we going to put the rest of them?' The king suggested where they could be stored. Meanwhile the princess, on seeing all this, was overjoyed as well as amazed, asking herself where it had all come from. The merchants, for their part, were delighted with what they had been given and they called down blessings on Ma'ruf. As for 'Ali, he started saying to himself in his astonishment: 'How did he manage to lie and cheat his way into the possession of all these treasures? If he had got them from the princess, he wouldn't have been giving them away to the poor. How fine are the lines of the poet:

> When the King of kings gives gifts,
> Do not ask the reason.
> God gives to whom He wants,
> So mind your manners.'

So much for him, but as for the king, he was astonished when he saw the lavish generosity with which Ma'ruf gave away money. Ma'ruf himself now went to his wife, who greeted him joyfully with smiles and laughter. She kissed his hand and said: 'Were you making fun of me or testing me when you told me that you were a poor man, running away from your wife? I praise God that I did not fall short in my duty to you, my darling, for whether you are rich or poor, there is no one dearer to me than you. Please tell me now what you meant by what you said.' Ma'ruf answered: 'I did mean to test you to see whether your love was genuine or merely a matter of money and a wish for worldly goods. You showed me your sincerity, and since you really love me, I welcome you and appreciate your integrity.'

He then went off by himself and rubbed the ring. Abu'l-Sa'adat appeared and said: 'Here I am; ask for what you want.' Ma'ruf told him: 'I want robes for my wife from a treasure chamber, as well as jewellery, including a necklace, set with forty incomparable gems.' 'To hear is to obey,' Abu'l-Sa'adat replied, and when he had fetched what he had been told to bring, Ma'ruf dismissed him and went with it to his wife. He placed the treasures in front of her, telling her that he wanted her to put them on, and when she saw them she was ecstatic with joy. Among them she found a pair of golden anklets studded with gems – the work of magicians – bracelets, earrings and a girdle, past all price. When she had put on the robe and this jewellery, she said: 'Master, I would like to keep these for feasts and holidays,' but he told her to wear them all the time, adding: 'I have plenty more besides them.' Her maids were delighted to see her wearing the robe and they kissed Ma'ruf's hands. He then left them and went off by himself to rub the ring. This time, when Abu'l-Sa'adat appeared, Ma'ruf told him to fetch a hundred robes together with jewellery. 'To hear is to obey,' said Abu'l-Sa'adat and he fetched the robes, each with its accompanying jewellery wrapped inside it. Ma'ruf took these and called for the maids. When they came, he presented one robe to each of them, with the result that, when they had put them on, they looked like the houris of Paradise, with the princess among them resplendent as the moon among stars. One of them told the king about this, and when he came to see his daughter, he found her and her maids dazzling all who looked at them.

Full of amazement, he went off, summoned the vizier and, after telling him what had happened, he added: 'What have you got to say to this?' 'King of the age,' replied the vizier, 'this is not the behaviour of a merchant. A merchant will sit for years hoarding pieces of linen and only sell them at a profit. How can men like that possibly acquire generous habits like these, and how can they get hold of wealth and jewels such as few kings possess or find themselves with quantities of goods like these? There must be something behind this, and if you will listen to me, I shall show you how to discover the truth.' The king agreed and the vizier went on: 'Arrange to meet him and then talk to him in a friendly way. Say: "I am thinking of going out to a garden to enjoy myself with nobody but you and the vizier." When we are there, we can set out wine and get him to drink. When he does that, he will lose his wits and his good sense, and if we then ask him how things really stand with him, he is bound to tell us what he is hiding, for wine gives secrets away. How well the poet has expressed it:

> When the effects of the wine I drank crept on their
>   way
> To where my secrets were, I cried out: "Stop!
>   Enough!"
> For fear of being overpowered, lest those
> Who drank with me might learn what I kept hid.

When he tells us the truth, we shall discover what he really is, and then we can do exactly what we want, for as things stand at the moment I am afraid of what could happen to you. He might want the throne for himself and win over the army by his lavish generosity, before deposing you and seizing power himself.' 'True enough,' said the king.

The two of them agreed on this plan that night. The next morning, the king went to his audience chamber and, as he was sitting there, his servants and grooms came to him in a state of distress. He asked them what was wrong and they told him: 'King of the age, the grooms rubbed down the horses and gave both them and the baggage mules their feed, but this morning we found that they had all been stolen by the mamluks. We searched the stables but saw no trace of them, and when we went to the mamluks' quarters we found them empty and we have no idea how they can have got away.' The king was astonished as he had thought that these had all been real – horses, mules, mamluks and all – not knowing that they were, in fact, *'auns* in the service of Abu'l-Sa'adat. 'Damn you,' he exclaimed, 'how can a thousand beasts, five hundred mamluks, and other servants as well, escape without anyone noticing?' They said that they could think of no answer, and so he told them: 'Go off and wait for your master to come out from the harem and then give him the news.' They went away and sat in dismay, until Ma'ruf came out and noticed how distressed they were. He asked the reason for this and they told him the news. He said: 'Were they so valuable that you should worry yourselves about them? Go off about your business.' He sat there laughing, showing no signs of anger or grief, while the king looked at the vizier and said: 'What kind of a man is this, for whom money has no value? There must be something behind this.'

They had talked for a while with him, when the king said: 'I want to go to a garden with the two of you to enjoy myself. What do you say?' Ma'ruf raised no objection and they went off to a garden which contained two kinds of every fruit, with flowing streams, tall trees and singing birds. They entered a pavilion that was calculated to clear sorrow from the heart, and there they sat talking, as the vizier told remarkable stories and amusing jokes, using language that stirred them to delight. Ma'ruf sat listening until the time came for their evening meal, when food was brought in as well as a pitcher of wine. After they had eaten and washed their hands, the vizier filled a wine cup, which he gave to the king, who drank it, and then, filling another, he said to Ma'ruf: 'Take wine, before whose dignity the heads of men's intelligence bow low.' 'What is it, vizier?' Ma'ruf asked, and the vizier said: 'This is the grey-haired virgin, long kept at home, who brings delight to men's hearts. It is of this that the poet has said:

> The barbarians' feet trampled it down,
> And it took its revenge on the heads of Arabs.
> It is poured by an infidel like the moon in darkness,
> Whose glances are the surest cause of sin.

How well another has expressed it in the lines:

> It is as though both wine and cupbearer,
> Who stands unveiling it among the guests,
> Danced like the morning sun, upon whose face
> The moon had placed twin stars as beauty spots.
> It is so delicate and subtly mixed
> That it flows through men's limbs like their souls.

Another good description is as follows:

> The moon of beauty clasped me all night long,
> Although the sun had not set in the glass.
> The fire to which the Magians bow down,
> Bowed down to me all night from the wine-jar.

Better than these are the lines of Abu Nuwas:

> Don't blame me, for this just prompts me to sin,
> But cure my sickness with what was its cause –
> Wine in whose courts sorrows cannot dismount;
> Its touch would fill a rock with happiness.
> In the dark night, as it rests in its jug,
> The house gleams with its glittering light.
> It passes among young men before whom Time is
>   humbled,

But what it does to them is only what they want,
Carried by a girl dressed as a boy,
The darling of sodomites and fornicators alike.
Tell the man who lays claim to knowledge:
"You may know something, but there is much you do
    not know."

How well another poet expressed it when he said:

This morning I'm the wealthiest of men,
Because I know that happiness will come.
For I have here a store of liquid gold,
Which I shall measure in a drinking cup.

Yet another has said:

The wine cup and the wine require respect;
It is their right that their rights be preserved.
When I am dead, bury me beside a vine;
It may be that its roots will wet my bones.
Don't lay me in the desert, for I fear
When I am dead that I may not taste wine.'

The vizier went on trying to persuade Ma'ruf to drink,
telling him of all the attractive qualities of wine, reciting
the lines written in its honour and telling him witty stories
until he was prompted to sip from the edge of the wine
cup. Soon this was all that he wanted, and as the vizier
kept on filling up the cup, he kept on drinking with such
pleasure that he became so fuddled that he could no longer
tell right from wrong. When the vizier saw that he had
passed the limits of sobriety and was completely drunk,
he said: 'Ma'ruf, I wonder where you got these unique
jewels. Not even the most powerful kings have any that
can match them and never in my life have I seen a

merchant who has acquired as much wealth as you have, nor one as generous as you. Your actions are those of a king and not of a merchant, and so, for God's sake, please tell me about yourself so that I may fully grasp the high position you occupy.' He went on wheedling away as best he could until Ma'ruf, who had now lost his wits completely, said: 'I am not a merchant or a king,' and went on to tell him his whole story from beginning to end. The vizier then pressed him to let him see the ring so that he could examine how it had been made, and in his drunken state Ma'ruf took it from his finger and handed it to him to inspect. The vizier took it and turned it over before saying: 'If I rub it, will the servant of the ring appear?' 'Yes, indeed,' Ma'ruf told him. 'He will come to you when you do that and you can then look at him.'

The vizier rubbed the ring and a voice spoke: 'Here am I, master. Ask, and your wish will be granted. Do you want a city destroyed or another built up, or do you want to have a king killed? I shall obediently do whatever you ask.' At that, the vizier pointed to Ma'ruf and said: 'Carry off this worthless creature and throw him down in the most desolate of deserts where he can find neither food nor drink, so that he may starve miserably to death without anyone knowing of his fate.' Abu'l-Sa'adat snatched up Ma'ruf and flew away with him between heaven and earth. Ma'ruf was sure that things were going to end badly, with his death, and he asked Abu'l-Sa'adat tearfully where he was taking him. He said: 'I am going to throw you down in the Empty Quarter, you ill-educated fellow. What man with a talisman like this can hand it to other people to look at? You deserve what has happened to you, and were it not for the fact that I fear God, I would drop you from a thousand fathoms up, so that before you

reached the ground the winds would blow you to pieces.'
He said nothing more until he reached the Empty Quarter,
where he dropped Ma'ruf and went off, leaving him alone
in the desert.

So much for Ma'ruf, but as for the vizier, when he got
hold of the ring, he said to the king: 'What do you think?
Didn't I tell you that he was a liar and a trickster and you
didn't believe me?' 'You were right, vizier, may God grant
you health,' the king said, 'and now let me look at the
ring.' The vizier turned to him angrily and spat in his face,
saying: 'You fool, why should I give it to you and remain
your servant, now that I have become your master. I am
not going to let you stay alive.' At that, he rubbed the ring
and when Abu'l-Sa'adat came, he said: 'Take this boor
and throw him down where you put his son-in-law, the
trickster.' So Abu'l-Sa'adat picked him up and as he was
carrying him off, the king said: 'Creature of God, what
crime have I committed?' 'I don't know,' answered Abu'l-
Sa'adat, 'but this is what my master ordered me to do and
I cannot disobey whoever holds the ring.' He flew on and
deposited the king in the same place as Ma'ruf, before
leaving him there and going back. Hearing the sound of
Ma'ruf weeping, the king went up to him and told him
what had happened. The two of them then sat shedding
tears for their misfortune, having nothing either to eat or
to drink.

This is what happened to them, but as for the vizier,
after getting rid of them both, he left the garden, assembled
all the troops and convened an assembly at which he told
them the story of the ring and let them know what he
had done with Ma'ruf and the king. He went on: 'Unless
you appoint me as your ruler, I shall order the servant of
the ring to carry all of you off and throw you into the

Empty Quarter to die of hunger and thirst.' 'Don't harm us,' they said, 'for we are content to accept you as our ruler and we shall not disobey your commands.' In this way, they were forced to submit to him and he gave them robes of honour. He then began to ask Abu'l-Sa'adat for whatever he wanted and this was immediately fetched for him.

He took his seat on the throne and, when he had received the homage of the troops, he sent a message to the princess, telling her: 'Prepare yourself, for I want you and am coming to lie with you tonight.' The princess burst into tears, finding it hard to bear the loss of her father and her husband, and she sent back to say: 'Wait for the end of the period that according to law I must delay after losing my husband, and you can then send me a note and sleep with me legally.' He wrote back: 'I don't recognize any waiting period, short or long. There is no need for letters; I see no difference between what is legal and what is not, and I shall certainly have you tonight.' At that, she sent back a letter welcoming him, but this was a trick on her part. The vizier was pleased and delighted to get her reply, as he was deeply in love with her. He ordered food to be provided for everyone, telling them: 'Eat; this is a wedding feast, for I propose to lie with the princess tonight.' The *shaikh* al-Islam objected that it was unlawful for him do this until the legal waiting period was over, after which a marriage contract could be drawn up, but he repeated: 'I don't recognize any waiting period; so say no more about it.' The *shaikh* was afraid that he might do him a mischief and so said nothing to him, but to the soldiers he said: 'This man is an irreligious unbeliever, a follower of no creed.'

That evening, the vizier went to the princess, whom

he found wearing her most splendid robes with her most magnificent ornaments. When she saw him, she went up to him laughingly and said: 'This is a blessed night, although I would have thought it even better had you killed my father and my husband.' 'I shall certainly do that,' he promised, after which she made him sit down and started to flirt with him, making a show of affection. When she talked caressingly to him, smiling at him, he became carried away, while for her part she was using this flattery to deceive him so that she could get hold of the ring and, in place of his joy, bring down misfortune on his head. In what she did she was following the advice of the poet who said:

By my cunning I achieved what I could not get by the
    sword,
And I came back with spoils which had been sweet to
    win.

When the vizier saw how tenderly she smiled at him, he felt a surge of passion and wanted to take her, but when he came near, she drew away and burst into tears. 'Sir,' she said, 'don't you see that man looking at us? For God's sake, keep me from his sight, for how can you make love to me while he is watching?' The vizier said angrily: 'Where is he?' and she said: 'In the ring; he is raising his head and looking at us.' The vizier laughed, thinking that the servant of the ring was watching them, and he said: 'Don't be afraid; this is the servant of the ring, who is under my control.' 'But I am afraid of '*ifrits*,' she objected, 'so take it off and throw it away from me.' He removed the ring and put it on the pillow before approaching her again, but when he did, she used her foot to give him such a kick that he fell over backwards, unconscious. She then called out to her servants, and when they hurried in she told them to seize him. While forty of her maids took hold of him, she quickly snatched the ring from the pillow and rubbed it. 'Here I am, mistress,' said Abu'l-Sa'adat, coming forward, and she told him: 'Take this infidel, put him in prison and load him with fetters.' So Abu'l-Sa'adat took the vizier to the Dungeon of Anger before returning to tell the princess.

She now asked him where he had taken her father and her husband, and when he told her that he had left them in the Empty Quarter, she ordered him to fetch them back immediately. 'To hear is to obey,' he said, and he then flew away and did not stop until he had reached the Empty Quarter, where he found the two of them sitting in tears and complaining to one another. 'Don't be afraid,' he called to them. 'Relief has come.' He told them what the vizier had done and explained: 'I imprisoned him with my own hands in obedience to my mistress's commands and she then instructed me to bring you back.' They were delighted by this news and Abu'l-Sa'adat flew off with them, bringing them back to the princess after no more than an hour. She rose to greet them, before seating them and producing food and sweetmeats. They spent the rest of the night with her and next morning she clothed them both in splendid robes and said to her father: 'Father, resume your seat on the royal throne but make my husband your chief vizier and tell the army what has happened. Then bring the old vizier out of prison, put him to death and burn the body. He was an infidel who wanted to lie with me by way of fornication rather than legal marriage, and he said himself that he was an unbeliever and a man of no religion. You must also be sure to treat your son-in-law well, now that you have appointed him as your chief vizier.' 'To hear is to obey, daughter,' her father replied, 'but give me the ring or else give it to your husband.' 'It is not for you or for him,' she said, adding: 'I will keep it and I shall probably guard it better than either of you. Whatever you want you can ask for from me and I shall then get the servant of the ring to fetch it for you. As long as I am alive and well you need fear no harm, and after my death you can do what you want with it.' 'That is the proper thing to do, my daughter,' her father agreed.

The king then went with Ma'ruf to the council chamber. His men had spent a troubled night because of the princess, as they were distressed to think that the vizier might have slept with her by way of fornication rather than after a legal marriage, and they were also concerned about the harm that he had done to the king and his son-in-law. They were afraid of a breach in Islamic law, as it was clear to them that the vizier was an unbeliever. When they assembled in the audience hall they began to criticize Shaikh al-Islam and ask him why he had not kept the vizier from fornication. His answer was: 'The man is an unbeliever, but he holds the ring and there is nothing that either you or I can do about him. God will repay him for what he has done, but meanwhile say nothing lest he kill you.' As they were gathered there talking, in came the king together with Ma'ruf, his son-in-law, and at this sight the soldiers rose to their feet delightedly and kissed the ground in front of him. After the king had taken his seat on his throne, he relieved their distress by telling them what had happened. On his orders the city was adorned with decorations and the vizier was taken from prison. As he passed the soldiers he was met with curses, insults and abuse and when he was brought before the king he was sentenced to be put to the most hideous of deaths.

He was killed and his body burned, while his wretched soul was consigned to hell. How well the poet's words describe him:

> May God's mercy shun the place where his bones lie,
> And may Munkar and Nakir never quit that spot.

Ma'ruf was now appointed as chief vizier, and things went well and happily for them all.

This went on for five years and then in the sixth the king died and the princess appointed Ma'ruf as his successor, but did not give him the ring. During this period she had conceived and given birth to a remarkably beautiful and perfectly formed son. The child stayed in the care of nurses until he was five years old, and it was then that his mother succumbed to a fatal illness. She sent for her husband and told him: 'I am ill.' 'May God make you well again, heart's darling,' he exclaimed, but she said: 'I may die,' adding: 'You don't need to be told to look after your son, but I must tell you to guard the ring, as I am afraid both for you and for him.' 'No harm can come to one whom God guards,' he told her, and at that she took off the ring and gave it to him. On the following day, she died and was gathered into the mercy of God, while Ma'ruf remained as king, administering the kingdom.

It happened that one day, after he had waved his handkerchief, sending his guards back to their own quarters, he went to his sitting room and sat there for the rest of the day until it grew dark. Then his leading courtiers arrived as usual to drink with him, and they stayed there, happily relaxing, until midnight. They then asked him for permission to leave and when this had been granted, they went off to their own homes. The maid whose duty it was to make up Ma'ruf's bed came in and spread out the mattress for him, before removing his robes and giving him his nightshirt. When he lay down, she began to massage his feet until he had fallen fast asleep, when she left him and went off to her own bed.

So much for her, but as for the sleeping Ma'ruf, he suddenly woke up in alarm to discover something beside him in the bed. He repeated the formula: 'I take refuge in God from the accursed devil,' before opening his eyes to discover an ugly woman lying beside him. 'Who are you?' he asked, and she said: 'Don't be alarmed; I am your wife, Dung Fatima.' When he looked at her he recognized her by her misshapen features and her long teeth. 'How did you get in here and who brought you to this country?' he asked. 'Where are you now?' she asked in return, and he said: 'In the city of Ikhtiyan al-Khutan,' adding: 'When did you leave Cairo?' 'This very hour,' she said, and when he asked her how that was, she explained: 'When I quarrelled with you and Satan tempted me to do you an injury, I lodged a complaint against you with the magistrates. They looked for you but could not find you and the *qadis* asked questions but failed to discover you. Two days passed and then I began to regret what I'd done, realizing that the fault was mine, but repentance did me no good. I sat for some days weeping over your departure. Then, as I was running short of money, I had to start begging for my bread from rich and poor alike, and, since you left me, it has only been in this humiliating way that I got any food at all. I was reduced to the worst of straits and every night I'd sit there weeping over your loss and lamenting the shame and humiliation, together with the misery and distress, that I had had to endure in your absence.'

Ma'ruf stared at her in astonishment as she started to tell him everything that had happened to her. She went on to say: 'I spent all yesterday going round begging, but nobody would give me anything and everyone whom I approached, asking for a crust, would hurl abuse at me and refuse to give me anything. When it grew dark I had to spend the night with nothing to eat, racked by hunger pangs, and, finding my sufferings hard to bear, I sat there in tears. At that moment, a figure appeared in front of me and said: "Woman, why are you weeping?" I replied: "I had a husband who used to spend money on me and do what I wanted, but I have lost him. I don't know where he went but since he left I have been unable to cope." He asked me the name of my husband and when I told him that it was Ma'ruf, he said: "I know the man. You must know that he is now the king of a city, and if you want, I shall take you to him." I said: "I appeal to you to do that," and he picked me up and flew off with me between heaven and earth until he brought me to this palace. "Go into this room," he said, "and there you will see your husband asleep on the bed." So I went in and found you in this lordly state. I hope that you will not abandon me, for I am your companion, and I praise God for reuniting me with you.' 'Did I leave you or did you leave me?' Ma'ruf asked. 'It was you who went from one *qadi* to another to complain about me, and to crown it all, you lodged a complaint against me with the High Court, setting the bailiff on me from the citadel so that I was forced to flee.'

He went on to tell her everything that had happened to him, explaining how he had become king after having married the princess, who had died, leaving a son who was now seven years old. Fatima said: 'What happened was predestined by the Almighty God. I have repented and I appeal to your honour not to abandon me. Let me eat my bread here with you as an act of charity.' She kept on abasing herself before him until he began to pity her. 'If you repent of your misdeeds,' he said, 'you can stay with me and you will be treated well, but if you try to harm me in any way, I shall have you killed. There is no one whom I fear, so you needn't think of complaining to the High Court and having the bailiff sent down from the citadel. I am now a king and people fear me, while I myself fear no one except Almighty God. I have a ring with which I can command the *jinn*, and when I rub it, its servant, Abu'l-Sa'adat, appears and brings me whatever I ask for. If you want to go back to Cairo, I shall provide you with money enough to last you for the rest of your life and send you back there quickly, but if you prefer to stay with me, I shall give you a palace of your own, furnish it with choice silks and assign twenty slave girls to wait on you. I shall provide you with regular supplies of delicious foods, as well as splendid robes, and you will live in the lap of luxury as a queen until either of us dies. What do you say to this?' 'I want to stay with you,' she told him and then she kissed his hand, repenting of her evil deeds.

He then gave her the sole use of a palace and presented her with slave girls and eunuchs, as she assumed the status of a queen. Ma'ruf's son used to visit both her and his father, but she disliked him as he was no son of hers, and when the boy saw her dislike and anger, he avoided her and returned her detestation. As for Ma'ruf, he was too busy paying court to beautiful slave girls to think about his wife, who had become an old woman whose scanty hair was grey and whose misshapen appearance was uglier than that of a spotted snake. Added to this was the fact that she had treated him as badly as possible, and, as the proverb has it: 'Ill treatment cuts off the roots of desire and sows hatred in the heart.' How well the poet has expressed it in the lines:

> Take care not to alienate the heart by wrongs;
> To win it back, when it has shied away, is hard.
> When love is lost, this heart becomes
> A broken glass that cannot be repaired.

It had not been for any laudable quality of hers that Ma'ruf had given her shelter, but rather this was a generous action through which he hoped to win the approval of Almighty God. Ma'ruf did not bother to sleep with Fatima.

When she saw that he was not going to approach her and was busying himself with other women, she hated him and was overcome by jealousy. At this point, Iblis inspired her with the idea of taking the ring from him, killing him and reigning as queen in his place. So one night she left her own apartments and went to those of her husband. As providence had decreed, Ma'ruf was sleeping with a lovely, graceful and shapely concubine. Before Fatima had left her quarters she had found out that when he wanted to make love, his piety would lead him to remove the ring from his finger, out of respect for the great names inscribed on it, and place it on the pillow, only putting it back on after he had ritually purified himself. He was also in the habit of dismissing his concubines out of fear for the ring, and when he went to the baths he would keep the door of his room locked until he returned and put it back on again, after which those who wanted could enter without hindrance.

All this Fatima knew, and so she came out at night in order to go in while he was fast asleep and to steal the ring without being seen. It so happened, however, that just as she did so, Ma'ruf's son had come out to relieve himself, carrying no light with him. As he was sitting in the dark on the seat of the privy, having left the door open, he caught sight of Fatima hurrying in the direction of his father's quarters. He said to himself: 'I wonder why this witch has left her own apartments in the dark of night and is heading for those of my father. There must be a reason behind this,' and he followed her, keeping out of sight. He had a short sword of polished steel, of which he was so proud that he never went to his father's court without it. His father used to laugh when he saw it and exclaim: 'Good God, that is a big sword you have, my son, but you have never yet taken it into battle or used it to cut off a head!' 'I shall certainly cut off one that deserves it,' he would say, and his father would laugh at his words. Now, while he was trailing Fatima, he drew this sword from its sheath and followed her until she went into his father's room. He stood by the door and watched as she searched, saying to herself: 'Where has he put the ring?' The prince realized what she was looking for, and waited for her to find it, until, with an exclamation – 'Here it is!' – she picked it up. As he hid behind the door she turned to leave the room and when she had come out, she looked at the ring and turned it over in her hand. She was just about to rub it when he raised his arm and struck her a blow on the neck with his sword. With a single shriek she fell down dead.

Ma'ruf was roused, seeing his wife lying in a pool of blood and his son with a drawn sword in his hand. 'What is this, my son?' he asked and the boy replied: 'How many times have you said: "That is a big sword you have, but you have never gone into battle with it or used it to cut off a head"? I would promise to cut off one that deserved

it, and now that is just what I have done for you.' He told
his father what had happened, and Ma'ruf started to look
for the ring. At first he couldn't find it but he kept on
searching Fatima's body until he noticed that her hand
was closed over it. He removed it and said: 'There is no
doubt at all that you are my true son. May God gladden
you, both in this world and the next, as you have saved
me from this vile woman whose only purpose was to
destroy me. How well the poet has expressed it:

> When God grants to a man His aid,
> Everything that he wants will come to him,
> But where this aid has been withheld,
> However hard he tries, he only harms himself.'

Ma'ruf now called out for his servants and when they
hurried in, he told them what his wife had done and
instructed them to take away her body and put it somewhere until morning. They did this, and then, on his
orders, a number of eunuchs took charge of it, washed it
and clothed it in a shroud. They made a tomb for her and
there she was buried, her journey from Cairo having
ended in her grave. How well the poet has put it:

> We travel on the path destined for us,
> And no man can avoid his destiny.
> Fate has decreed where we are going to die,
> And no one dies in any other land.

Another poet expressed it well when he wrote:

> When I go out to look for fortune in a land,
> I do not know which of two fates will follow;
> It may be that the good I seek will come,
> Or else misfortune may be seeking me.

After this, Ma'ruf sent for the peasant who had entertained him when he was a fugitive, and when the man came he appointed him as his chief vizier and counsellor. As Ma'ruf discovered, he turned out to have a beautiful daughter, who combined good qualities with a distinguished lineage and an excellent reputation. He married her and after a time he found a wife for his son. They continued to enjoy the most prosperous, pleasant and enjoyable of lives until they were visited by the destroyer of delights, the parter of companions, the ravager of prosperous lands, who orphans children. Praise be to the Living God, Who never dies and in Whose hand are the keys of dominion and power.

When she had finished telling this story to King Shahriyar, Shahrazad, seeing it was not yet light, began to recount the story we are now going to hear . . .

Glossary

Many of the Arabic terms used in the translation are to be found in *The Oxford English Dictionary*. Of these the commonest – 'emir' and 'vizier', for instance – are not entered in italics in the text and, in general, are not glossed here.

Abu Nuwas   Abu Nuwas al-Hasan ibn Hani (*c.*755–*c.*813), a famous, or notorious, poet of the 'Abbasid period, best known for his poems devoted to love, wine and hunting.

'Atiya   *see* Jarir ibn 'Atiya

'aun   a powerful *jinni*.

dinar   a gold coin. It can also be a measure of weight.

Fatiha   literally, the 'opening'; the first *sura* (chapter) of the Quran.

ghul   a cannibalistic monster. A *ghula* is a female *ghul*.

houri   a nymph of the Muslim Paradise. Also a great beauty.

Iblis   the devil.

'ifrit   a kind of *jinni*, usually evil; an *'ifrita* is a female *jinni*.

Jarir ibn 'Atiya   (d. 729) a leading poet of the Umaiyad period, famous for his panegyric and invective verse.

jinni   a (male) spirit in Muslim folklore and theology; *jinniya* is a female spirit. *Jinn* (the collective term) assumed various forms: some were servants of Satan, while others were good Muslims and therefore benign.

Joseph   features in the Quran as well as the Bible. In the Quran, he is celebrated for his beauty.

Ka'ba   the cube-shaped holy building in Mecca to which Muslims turn when they pray.

khan   an inn, caravanserai or market.

Maghribi   an inhabitant of the region of North Africa between the Atlas Mountains and the Mediterranean (in modern usage the area now covered by Morocco, Algeria and Tunisia).

Magian   a Zoroastrian, a fire worshipper. In the *Nights*, the Magians invariably feature as sinister figures.

mamluk   slave soldier. Most mamluks were of Turkish origin.

marid   a type of *jinni*.

Munkar and Nakir   two angels who examine the dead in their tombs and, if necessary, punish them.

nusf   literally, 'a half '; a small coin.

qadi   a Muslim judge.

qintar   a measure of weight, variable from region to region, equivalent to 100 *ratls*.

ratl   a measure of weight, varying from region to region.

Rum   theoretically designates Constantinople and the Byzantine lands more generally, but in some stories the name is merely intended to designate a strange and usually Christian foreign land.

Shaddad ibn 'Ad   legendary king of the tribe of 'Ad who attempted to build the city of Iram as a rival to Paradise and was punished by God for his presumption.

shaikh   a tribal leader, the term also commonly used to refer to an old man or a master of one of the traditional religious sciences or a leader of a dervish order. Similarly, a *shaikha* is an old woman or a woman in authority.

POPULAR PENGUINS

FICTION

POPULAR PENGUINS

NON-FICTION